The Fortune-Teller's Secret

Madame Destiny flipped over one card, then another, without uttering a word.

"Did the spirits run out of things to say about me?" Nancy asked with a grin.

The fortune-teller glared at her. "You shouldn't make light of the spirits," she warned in an icy voice. "They are very, very powerful."

Madame Destiny continued flipping cards. "I see that you are in some sort of investigation profession. Perhaps you are a police officer—or a private detective?"

Nancy's eyes widened. How did Madame Destiny know that?

Without waiting for Nancy's response, Madame Destiny turned over another card—and gasped.

On it was a picture of a skeleton holding a scythe. Above the skeleton was a single word: Death.

Nancy Drew
Mystery Stories

Available from MINSTREL Books

NANCY DREW MYSTERY STORIES®

121

NANCY DREW®

THE FORTUNE-TELLER'S SECRET

CAROLYN KEENE

A
MINSTREL®
BOOK

PUBLISHED BY POCKET BOOKS

New York   London   Toronto   Sydney   Tokyo   Singapore

A MINSTREL PAPERBACK *Original*

A Minstrel Book published by
POCKET BOOKS, a division of Simon & Schuster Inc.
1230 Avenue of the Americas, New York, NY 10020

Copyright © 1994 by Simon & Schuster Inc.
Produced by Mega-Books of New York, Inc.

ISBN: 0-671-87204-4

First Minstrel Books printing October 1994

10 9 8 7 6 5 4 3 2 1

NANCY DREW, NANCY DREW MYSTERY STORIES, A MINSTREL BOOK and colophon are registered trademarks of Simon & Schuster Inc.

Cover art by Aleta Jenks

Printed in the U.S.A.

Contents

1

A Suspicious Death

Bess Marvin's eager blue eyes swept over the crowded fairgrounds. "Where do you want to start, guys?" she asked. "How about the apple cider stand? Or maybe the maple sugar ice cream stand?"

Nancy Drew and George Fayne exchanged a grin. "We should probably find Yasmine before we hit the food booths," Nancy said to Bess. "We came to the Harvest Festival to meet her, remember?"

Eighteen-year-old Nancy brushed back a strand of reddish blond hair and peered at her watch. "In fact, I told her we'd meet her by the information booth at two. Come on, let's get moving."

As the three of them started strolling, Nancy noted that the place was buzzing with activity.

1

Off to the right were pens with goats, pigs, and other animals for children to pet. To the left, a group of people were demonstrating folk dances. In addition, there were dozens of booths selling food and gifts: apples, pumpkins, breads, and cheeses, and handmade pottery, baskets, and jewelry.

"It'll be great to see Yasmine, won't it?" George remarked. She stepped aside to make way for a group of girls eating sticky-looking clouds of cotton candy. "It's been ages since she was our counselor at summer camp."

"Remember how many neat things she showed us on our nature hikes?" Bess said. "I bet she's acing her premed classes at Westmoor."

"Nancy! Bess! George! Over here!" a familiar voice called out.

Nancy and her friends spotted their friend Yasmine Nasser waiting near the information booth just ahead, smiling and waving. She was exactly as Nancy remembered her: tall and wiry, with shoulder-length, curly brown hair, olive skin, and large hazel eyes. She was wearing jeans and a gray, hooded Westmoor University sweat-shirt.

"I'm so glad you all could make it," Yasmine said after a round of hugs.

"You, too," Nancy said, her blue eyes spar-kling. "How did you manage to take a Friday afternoon off, with school and everything?"

"I don't have any classes on Fridays, and I'm all caught up on my lab work," Yasmine explained. "I figured I deserved a little outing with my old friends. And my boyfriend, too," she added. "Craig will be meeting us here—I'm not sure when."

"Wow, you've got a boyfriend!" Bess said eagerly. "How long have you two been dating?"

"Four months, two weeks, and three days," Yasmine replied, blushing slightly. "I'm kind of crazy about him—can you tell?"

"You mentioned him on the phone," Nancy said. "You met him at the city animal shelter, right?"

"Yup. We're both volunteers there," Yasmine said, then added, "Hey, speaking of animals, should we take in some of this stuff? We can catch up while we walk around."

The girls began wandering through the fairgrounds, chattering the whole way. It was a beautiful day to be outdoors: warm and sunny, with just a touch of autumn chill.

"Why don't we sit and rest for a bit?" Bess suggested, pointing to a sunny patch of grass nearby. "My feet are killing me!"

"How can your feet be killing you?" George asked in disbelief. "We've only been here half an hour."

"It's these shoes." Bess plopped down on the grass and wriggled her feet. She had on bright

3

red ankle boots with high, pointy heels. "They're kind of hard to move around in."

George rolled her eyes. "Then why did you wear them? Why don't you get some sensible shoes, like mine?" She stuck out a foot to show off her thick-soled leather hiking boots.

Yasmine leaned toward Nancy and whispered, "I keep forgetting they're cousins."

Nancy laughed. She knew exactly what Yasmine meant. George and Bess were as different as night and day. George was passionate about sports, while Bess avoided physical activity whenever possible. They were opposites in appearance, too. Bess was petite, with long, straw blond hair, while tall, athletic George had brown eyes and short, curly dark hair.

As the other three settled on the grass beside Bess, their attention was drawn to a nearby booth, where a crowd of people had gathered. "No More Bugs is one hundred percent guaranteed to eliminate those pesky insects that love to chew up your indoor and outdoor plants," the salesman was saying in an animated patter. "And if you consider how much money you spend replacing your damaged plants, No More Bugs is a downright bargain!"

"What a sales pitch," George said skeptically. "The stuff is probably ground-up chalk or something."

"That reminds me of an article I read the other

day in *Crime Today*," Nancy said. "It was about con artists."

"Con artists?" George repeated. "You mean crooks who take people's money for phony investment deals, insurance scams, stuff like that?"

Nancy nodded. "Phony products, too. This article said that some guy was selling a really expensive bug killer through the mail. A lot of people sent in money for it, and all they got was a cheap plastic flyswatter."

Bess whistled. "Did the guy go to jail?"

"Nope," Nancy replied. "He shut down his operation before the authorities caught up to him. None of the people ever got any money back. Con artists can be pretty slippery." She suddenly noticed that Yasmine had turned pale and was staring at the ground. "Yasmine? Are you okay?"

When Yasmine looked up, Nancy saw that her hazel eyes were troubled. "I was just thinking about this woman I know—Frances Kittredge," Yasmine explained. "She's been our next-door neighbor for years. When you started talking about con artists . . ."

"Did this Frances person get ripped off by a con artist?" George asked curiously.

Yasmine brushed an ant off her jeans. "I'm not sure," she said slowly. "But she's been acting weird ever since her husband, Jake, died last April."

"But isn't that normal, under the circumstances?" Bess piped up. "I mean, Frances is probably still grieving, right?"

"That's true," Yasmine admitted. "Frances and Jake *were* incredibly devoted to each other. But her behavior—well, I have a feeling there's more to it than grief."

Nancy sat up slightly. She was an amateur detective, and her keen instincts were aroused by Yasmine's story. "Go on," she urged.

"I used to spend a lot of time at their house," Yasmine explained, sounding wistful. "Frances was always really nice to me. She would bake every Saturday and invite me over to sample whatever she was making. It was very—well, grandmotherly. Both my grandmothers are dead."

"I'm sorry, Yasmine," Nancy said softly. Her own mother had died when she was three years old, and she sympathized.

"Anyway, after Jake died, Frances totally changed," Yasmine went on. "She started ignoring me, and the Saturday baking stopped. Then, one Saturday a while ago, I noticed something odd."

"What?" George prodded.

Yasmine gazed up at the sky. "I got this idea to drop by her house, just to make sure she was okay. She was on her way out, and she told me she didn't have time to talk to me. I felt hurt, but I

6

didn't say anything. But then I happened to spot something sticking out of her purse—an envelope, with money in it. A lot of money."

"Like how much?" Bess asked, her eyes wide.

"It looked like a fat wad of brand-new twenty-dollar bills," Yasmine said. "I was curious, but I didn't want to be nosy, so I didn't say anything. But then the next Saturday, I was in the yard exercising my dogs, and I saw Frances go out again—at exactly the same time, around noon. And it happened again the Saturday after that."

George leaned forward. "Did you ever ask Frances where she was going on these Saturdays?"

"I did, a few days ago," Yasmine said. "She got nervous and clammed up. It was *very* weird."

"And you think there's a con artist in the picture," Nancy concluded.

Yasmine shrugged helplessly. "It's just a hunch. But from what I've heard about con artists, she's definitely a prime target. She's old, she's a widow, and she's probably got a bit of savings. I figure she must have gotten some life insurance money when Jake died, too. She's been acting so weird—do you suppose she might be paying money to some crook every week? Like for a bogus investment scheme or something?"

Nancy looked thoughtful. "I'd be happy to check it out for you, Yasmine."

Yasmine's eyes lit up. "Would you, Nancy? That would be fantastic. I've been so worried."

"Could you arrange for me to meet her as soon as possible? Without telling her what I'm up to, that is," Nancy asked.

"Absolutely," Yasmine said. "Why don't you girls come by my house after dinner, and we'll all go over there?"

Just then a male voice rang out. "Yasmine!" Nancy looked up. A tall, cute guy in his early twenties was rushing toward them, down the aisle between the booths. He had a long, lean face, steel gray eyes, and dirty blond hair that curled over the collar of his brown leather jacket.

He knelt down by Yasmine and kissed her on the cheek. "I'm sorry I couldn't get away sooner," he said. "I hope you haven't missed me too much."

"I always miss you when you aren't around," Yasmine said, beaming. Then she turned to the three girls. "Nancy, Bess, George—this is Craig Chandler, my boyfriend."

"Nice to meet you all," Craig said cheerfully, then glanced around. "Great fair, isn't it?"

"Actually, we've only seen a little bit of it," George replied.

"We've been hanging out here talking about Frances," Yasmine explained to Craig. "Nancy's going to help me find out if she's in trouble."

To Nancy's surprise, Craig frowned. "Oh . . . really?" He didn't sound too happy.

Yasmine looked puzzled. "Is something wrong, Craig?"

Craig was silent for a moment, then he shook his head and smiled at Yasmine. "No, nothing's wrong." He turned to Nancy. "It's very nice of you to help out."

"Oh, I'm glad to do it," Nancy said. She was a little confused by Craig's reaction to the fact that she would be working on the case. But she brushed her confusion aside and decided to ask Yasmine more questions about her elderly friend.

"So, Yasmine, you said that Frances's husband died in April, right?" Nancy said. "Was he sick?"

"Not at all," Yasmine replied. "Jake died in a boating accident upstate, at Lake Sacandaga. He and Frances were out in their boat, and he slipped and fell overboard. She dived into the water and tried to save him, but he never resurfaced." She shuddered. "His body was never found."

"That's terrible!" Bess cried out.

"What's really terrible is that Jake was a terrific swimmer," Yasmine went on. "The police thought that he might have been knocked unconscious before he hit the water—maybe he banged his head on the edge of the boat."

Nancy silently digested this information. The

9

circumstances of Jake's death seemed odd to her, but her thoughts were interrupted as Craig jumped to his feet. "Anyone want something to drink? Some apple cider?" he said briskly.

"I'll go with you," Yasmine offered, standing up. "We can get cider for everybody."

After they left, George turned to Nancy. "How are you going to find out if Frances is being hounded by a con artist, Nan?"

Nancy leaned back on her elbows. "Maybe there's more to this story than a possible con artist," she said thoughtfully.

Bess frowned. "Like what?"

"A couple of things don't add up," Nancy replied. "First of all, Frances's husband was a terrific swimmer, yet he drowned—and his body never turned up." She paused. "I hate to say it, but what if there was foul play?"

"Foul play?" George repeated. "You mean—as in murder?"

Nancy nodded grimly. "Exactly."

2

A Shadow in the Hallway

"Murder!" Bess cried out.

"It's just a theory," Nancy told her quickly. "But it's a theory we have to consider, especially if Jake's body was never found."

"But then how do you explain Frances's strange behavior all these months?" George spoke up.

"Let's see," Nancy said, sitting up. "Frances takes off to some mysterious destination at the same time every Saturday, and she won't tell Yasmine where she's going. And at least one of those times, she had an envelope full of money with her." She shook her head. "Maybe Yasmine's right and Frances is the victim of a con artist or . . . she could be paying off a blackmailer."

"A blackmailer?" Bess echoed. "But why

would she be paying off a blackmailer, unless . . ." Her blue eyes grew enormous. "Unless *she* murdered Jake—to collect the life insurance money? Maybe somebody saw the whole thing and started demanding lots of money to keep quiet."

"That's silly," George scoffed. "Why would Frances kill Jake? Yasmine said they were devoted to each other."

Nancy held up one hand. "Shh, you guys—here come Yasmine and Craig. I don't want to upset her with any premature conclusions. We need to get more facts before going any further."

Besides, she thought to herself, she didn't want to let Craig in on the investigation. Even though he was Yasmine's boyfriend, he sure had acted strangely when they were talking about Frances a few minutes before.

Yasmine and Craig walked up with cups of apple cider and a bag of freshly baked pretzels. The five of them sat on the grass and chatted while they ate and drank. Then they got up and began touring the rest of the fairgrounds.

At one point Nancy found herself alone with Craig, standing under a fiery red maple tree while Yasmine, George, and Bess went off to dunk for apples.

"So, Nancy," Craig said. "What's your plan of action? Regarding Frances Kittredge, that is."

Nancy studied him curiously. What was his interest in Frances? "I don't have one yet," she told him carefully. To keep Craig from asking her any more questions about the case, she changed the subject. "Are you a student at Westmoor, too?"

Craig looked away. "Um, no," he muttered, sounding uncomfortable. "I'm in the restaurant business."

"Really?" Nancy said. "And what do you—"

"Hey, Nan! I got a prize!" Bess rushed up to them, with George and Yasmine at her heels. The girls' faces were shiny and wet, and their hair clung damply to their foreheads.

Bess held up a small stuffed cow. "I dunked six apples in less than a minute!" she announced proudly. "Aren't I amazing?"

George grinned mischievously at her. "I think you were just hungry."

Bess glared at her cousin. "You're just jealous because I won something and you didn't."

The five of them spent the next few hours enjoying the rest of the fair. It was after dark when they finally stood in the parking lot by Nancy's blue Mustang, saying goodbye.

"That was so much fun." Bess sighed, unloading an armful of purchases into the backseat. In addition to her stuffed cow, she had bought a blackberry pie, a jar of pear jelly, and a russet-red Harvest Festival T-shirt.

Craig gave Yasmine's hand a lingering squeeze. "I'll see you later," he told her softly. Then he waved at the other girls. "Nice meeting you all." He turned and started across the lot, a ring of keys jingling in his hand.

Yasmine smiled as she watched him walk away, but her expression changed as she turned back to the girls. "About the case," she said quickly. "Can you all come by my house tonight—say, around eight or eight-thirty? I can take you over to meet Frances then. She's usually home in the evening."

"No problem," Nancy said, and George and Bess nodded in agreement.

Looking across the parking lot just then, Nancy noticed Craig unlocking the door of a small yellow convertible. She knew the model—it was a pricey one.

He must be doing awfully well in the restaurant business to be able to afford such a fancy car, Nancy mused.

At six o'clock Nancy, George, and Bess stepped into the Drews' front hallway. The mouth-watering smells of roast chicken and mashed potatoes greeted them.

Without taking off her jacket, Nancy headed straight for the kitchen. Hannah Gruen was at the sink, making a tossed green salad. Nancy felt a rush of affection for the gray-haired housekeeper, who had helped raise her since her mother died.

"Hi, Hannah," Nancy called out. "Guess what?"

Hannah turned around and grinned. "You caught a gang of jewel thieves this afternoon, and the mayor is going to give you a medal."

Nancy laughed. "No, silly. I brought Bess and George over for dinner—I hope that's okay."

"Of course," Hannah replied heartily.

Bess poked her head in the kitchen and held up the blackberry pie from the Harvest Festival. "We even brought our own dessert, Hannah."

"A pie—wonderful!" Hannah exclaimed. "We can put it in the oven to warm and serve it with vanilla ice cream."

Twenty minutes later Hannah and the girls sat down to dinner, along with Nancy's father.

"How was your day?" Carson Drew asked Nancy as he spooned some mashed potatoes onto his plate. Carson, a renowned criminal lawyer, was in his forties. He had dark brown hair and eyes the same color blue as his daughter's.

"Great," Nancy replied, and proceeded to tell him all about the fair and seeing Yasmine.

Carson passed the carrots to Bess. "So Yasmine thinks Frances is getting duped by a con artist, eh?" he said to Nancy. "One of my clients was taken in by a con, not long ago."

"Really, Dad?" Nancy said eagerly. Her father

15

often provided her with useful leads. "Can you talk about it?"

Carson nodded. "Her name's Edwina Leidig. She's a widow in her late sixties, fairly well-to-do. Some man convinced her to put a lot of money into one of his investment ventures—"

"And the venture turned out to be phony," Nancy finished. "Did you manage to get her money back for her?"

"I'm afraid not," Carson admitted. "The man seems to have disappeared into thin air. The police are on the case now."

Nancy lapsed into a thoughtful silence. After a moment, she said, "Maybe I should speak to Mrs. Leidig, Dad. If Frances really is being taken in by a con artist, there could be a chance it's the same guy who stole Mrs. Leidig's money."

"Sounds like a smart plan to me," Carson said. "Why don't I give Edwina a call after dinner?"

Over the phone, Edwina Leidig agreed to see Nancy that evening. At eight, Nancy, Bess, and George were ringing the doorbell of a large yellow Victorian house.

The door was opened by a slender woman with a snowy white pageboy and bright green eyes. She blinked at Nancy and said, "You must be Carson's daughter. You look just like him."

Nancy smiled, then introduced George and

16

Bess. "Thanks for agreeing to see us, Mrs. Leidig."

"Please, call me Edwina," the older woman said with a smile.

Edwina ushered them into her living room. A crystal vase of pink roses stood on an antique coffee table. An enormous black-and-white cat lay sleeping on one of the gold brocade couches.

"Roberto, bad boy, you know you're not allowed to sit there," she scolded him, but she made no effort to move him. She sat and fixed her kindly gaze on Nancy. "Now, what can I do for you?"

Perching on a sofa, Nancy took a deep breath. "We're worried that someone we know may be getting taken in by a con artist," she began. "And my father thought you might be able to—"

Edwina raised a hand. "Say no more," she said. Nancy noticed that a blush had crept into her cheeks. "I don't like talking about what happened to me—I feel like such a fool! But I'll tell you girls, if it'll help your friend."

She lifted Roberto onto her lap and began petting him. "Two months ago," she said, "a man named Thomas Whittle from a company called Capital Appreciation, Inc., called me up, out of the blue. He wanted me to put three thousand dollars into what he called a surefire real estate venture."

17

"What kind of real estate venture?" Nancy asked her curiously.

"He said they were buying up houses that lay in the path of a new freeway the state was planning. Then, when the government wanted to buy the land to build in the highway, they could sell the houses at an enormous profit," Edwina replied.

"Did you invest your money?" Nancy asked.

Edwina nodded. "Yes. And within a month, I had doubled my initial investment. I thought I was onto something big, so I gave Mr. Whittle more money—ten thousand this time. Needless to say, I never saw the money again. The next time I called, Capital Appreciation had disconnected its phone."

"Wow," George murmured sympathetically. "Have the police gotten any leads on Thomas Whittle?"

Edwina shook her head sadly. "They haven't been able to find any trace of Mr. Whittle or his company—or my ten thousand dollars."

Nancy asked her a few more questions, then rose to go. "Thanks for telling us about this."

"You're very welcome," Edwina replied. "I just hope that Mr. Whittle is caught before he steals from anybody else."

As the girls drove to Yasmine's, George said, "So what do you think, Nan? Could there be any connection between Edwina's situation and Frances's?"

Nancy steered smoothly around a tight corner. "There's no way to tell at this point," she said. "For all we know, there's nothing fishy at all going on with Frances—no con artists, no blackmailers, nothing."

She added, "Of course, there's still the business with her husband's death. I'd like to find out more about that. Maybe I'll call up the Lake Sacandaga Village police tomorrow and get a copy of the accident report."

After a few minutes they found the Nassers' place—a large modern house of white stucco and glass brick. The front yard was landscaped with dramatically lit rocks and miniature trees.

Yasmine sat on the porch poring over a biology textbook. "Hi," she called out, looking up and snapping the book shut.

Nancy, Bess, and George got out of the Mustang and joined Yasmine on the porch steps.

"Frances is home," Yasmine said, nodding toward the square gray stone house next door. "That's her car in the driveway. But I was just thinking—we should come up with an excuse for why I wanted you guys to meet her. What do you all think of this plan. . . ."

Five minutes later the girls were ringing Frances's buzzer. The door was opened by a plump, elderly woman. The red plaid robe she wore set off her short, silvery gray curls.

Her pale blue eyes darted anxiously from Yasmine to the other girls. "I was just sitting down to my program," she said uneasily.

"I'm sorry to interrupt you, Frances," Yasmine spoke up cheerfully. "But I wanted to introduce you to these friends of mine."

"Nancy, George, and I really love dogs," Bess added brightly. "When Yasmine told us that you had a Chinese crusty—"

"Crested," George cut in quickly, smiling at Frances. "A Chinese crested. When Yasmine told us you had one, we just had to come over and see it."

"You want to see my Ariel?" Frances raised her eyebrows. She paused, then said reluctantly, "Well, just for a minute, then."

Frances showed them into a cozy den with overstuffed couches and chairs, an upright piano, and nautical art on the walls. She stood in the doorway and clapped her hands. "Ariel!" she said loudly. "Ar-i-el!"

"You have a beautiful place, Mrs. Kittredge," Nancy told her, leaning against the piano.

"Thank you, dear," Frances said hastily. "Where *is* that dog? Ariel!"

Frances seems skittish and tense, Nancy thought. Maybe Yasmine was right—maybe Frances did have something to hide.

Several framed photographs stood on top of the piano. Nancy picked one up. It showed a handsome gray-haired man standing at the helm of a sailboat, with the name *Prospero* painted on its bow.

"That's my husband," she heard Frances say. "That *was* my husband."

Nancy glanced up. Frances didn't seem skittish or tense any longer, just sad. "I'm sorry," she said softly, putting the photo back.

"He loved that boat," Frances added, her voice trembling.

At that moment a small dog came trotting into the room. Nancy had never seen anything like it. It was hairless except for a feathery crest on its head and a few sparse plumes on its feet and at the end of its tail.

"Hello, Ariel," Bess murmured, reaching out to pet it. It sniffed her fingers, then growled.

"Gee, Bess, you sure have a way with animals," George teased.

"Ariel isn't used to strangers," Yasmine told them. "But she knows me—don't you, Ariel, sweetie?" she cooed, scratching its nose.

While her friends were fussing over the dog, Nancy turned her attention back to Frances. "Why is your boat called the *Prospero?*" she asked her.

Frances hesitated, then said, "Jake used to be an amateur actor—Shakespeare, mostly.

21

Prospero's a character in his favorite play, *The Tempest*. Ariel is named after a character in the play, too. Do you know *The Tempest*, dear? Or don't you young people read Shakespeare anymore?"

Nancy was about to reply, but then something caught her eye.

In the hallway just outside the den, a dark shadow had fallen across the wall.

Someone's out there, Nancy realized with a shiver. Who was eavesdropping on her conversation with Frances?

3

Hot on the Trail

Nancy stared warily at the doorway. She was
about to ask Frances if she had other company,
when the shadow moved and a woman walked
into the room.

Nancy studied her curiously. She was tall and
slender, with short platinum blond hair and dark
brown eyes, and appeared to be in her forties.
She was dressed in a black designer jogging suit
and expensive white sneakers. She carried a
clothing catalog in one hand and a steaming mug
of tea in the other.

After glancing at Nancy and the other girls, the
woman stared pointedly at Frances. "I gotta talk
to you," she said in a low voice. Nancy thought
she could detect a southern accent. "Right
away," the woman added. Then, without another
word, she marched back into the hallway.

23

Frances frowned, muttered, "Excuse me," and followed the woman.

Nancy turned to Yasmine. "Who was that?" she whispered.

"That's Frances's live-in housekeeper," Yasmine whispered back. "Loretta—Loretta Hart."

After a moment Frances came back into the den. She seemed upset.

"You're all going to have to leave now," she said, wringing her hands. "I, er . . . something's come up. Please, you have to go."

Yasmine touched Frances's arm. "Are you okay? Is there anything I can do?"

Frances stepped back from her and shook her head vigorously. "No, no, dear, I'm fine. Please, you'll have to excuse me now."

Yasmine gazed helplessly at Nancy. Nancy shrugged, then turned to Frances, who was staring blankly at the floor, deep in thought.

What had Loretta said to change her mood so drastically? Nancy wondered. Frances hadn't exactly been warm and welcoming before, but now she was practically pushing them out of the house.

"Thanks for showing us Ariel," Nancy said. Frances nodded without even looking up.

As soon as the girls were outside, Bess made a face and said, "Can someone tell me what just hap—"

Nancy put a finger to her lips. "Let's talk at Yasmine's," she whispered.

The four of them walked in silence across the yard to Yasmine's house. It was a bleak, chilly night, and Nancy crossed her arms over her chest, trying to keep warm.

She had no idea what to think about Frances now. It was hard to believe that she could have murdered Jake for the insurance money— Frances had seemed genuinely sad about her husband's death. But if she wasn't being blackmailed, then where was she going every Saturday with a purse full of cash?

And the scene just now with Loretta Hart looked suspicious, too, Nancy reflected. What had the housekeeper said to Frances to upset her so much? Nancy determined to find out more about Loretta from Yasmine.

When Yasmine opened the front door of her house, three large brown dogs jumped up on her immediately, barking and panting happily. "Hi, Izzy. Hi, Boots. Hi, Cleopatra," Yasmine called out, laughing and rubbing their ears. "I got these dogs from the animal shelter, when they were still puppies," she explained to the girls. "They're sisters. Someone abandoned them near the railroad tracks. Who could do such a thing?"

"You were nice to take them in," Bess told her. "Three of them—wow! They must be a lot of work."

"Oh, they're not so bad," Yasmine said, giving Cleopatra an extra pat. "And I had to take all three—I couldn't bear to break up the family.

"I just hope they get along with cats," she added, wincing. "I'm thinking of adopting this litter of four kittens I saw at the shelter. They need a home, too—the poor little cats look so helpless."

Yasmine led them into the Nassers' sleek, modern living room. Beige leather-and-chrome chairs were clustered around an exquisite Persian rug. On the slate coffee table Nancy spotted several silver and turquoise scarabs. She leaned over to look at them.

"My parents brought those over from Egypt a long time ago, when they moved to this country," Yasmine remarked as they settled on the couch.

"Speaking of your parents, are they around?" George asked her.

Yasmine shook her head. "They're in Paris for the week, attending a conference. They both travel a lot on business." Nancy thought she looked a little sad saying this.

Nancy leaned forward. "Tell me about Loretta, Yasmine," she prompted her friend.

"Loretta's been the Kittredges' housekeeper for about three years," Yasmine said, smoothing back her dark curls. "She's never been real friendly to me. I don't know a whole lot about her."

"Can you guess why Frances became so eager for us to leave after she and Loretta talked?" Nancy persisted.

Yasmine shrugged. "I have no idea. That was weird, wasn't it? But Frances has been like that since Jake died—moody and unpredictable. I never know what she's going to say or do next."

George reached down to pet one of the dogs, who were sitting contentedly on the Persian rug. "Frances is healthy, right?" she asked Yasmine. "I mean, you don't think she's been acting funny because she's sick or something?"

"Good question, George," Nancy said, nodding. "How about it, Yasmine?"

"I kind of doubt that's what's going on," Yasmine replied. "Frances has always been healthy as a horse. She used to love to brag about how everybody in her family—the Paretsky family—lived to a ripe old age."

"Let's get back to your theory about there being a con artist in the picture, Yasmine," Nancy said. "You mentioned something about life insurance money. Do you know if Jake Kittredge definitely had a policy? And if so, do you know if Frances got paid anything?"

"I'm sure he had a policy," Yasmine said firmly. "I heard him complaining to Frances once about how much the policy cost. As for whether the check ever came through . . ." She looked thoughtful. "I really have no idea. And I don't see any way of finding out, unless we ask Frances outright."

The girls talked for a little while longer, then Nancy glanced at her watch. "It's late; we'd better call it a night. Tomorrow's going to be a big day."

Bess raised her eyebrows. "Why, Nan?"

"It's Saturday," Nancy said, "the day Frances makes her weekly outing."

"You didn't tell me this surveillance stuff would be so boring," Bess grumbled. "Not to mention the fact that I had to get up at the crack of dawn!"

Nancy and Bess were sitting in the front seat of Nancy's Mustang, parked across the street and a few houses down from Frances's place.

Nancy took a sip of orange juice from a carton. "I wanted to get here early, in case Frances happened to change her schedule," she explained patiently. She rummaged through a white paper bag. "Here, how about an onion bagel? Maybe that'll cheer you up."

"Oh, I guess," Bess said wearily. She took a bite. "Mmm. Not bad." She chewed for a moment, then added, "I have to admit, this is better than that fifteen-kilometer race George is running. It looks like rain, too—I bet George gets soaked."

Nancy peered at the dashboard clock. "Ten-thirty," she murmured. "If all goes according to plan, Frances will be coming out the front door in about an hour and—hey, there she is! Bess, get down!" Nancy ducked her head below the dashboard.

Bess quickly jammed her half-eaten bagel in her mouth and slouched down. "Whas haffening?" she whispered, half choking on her bagel.

Nancy raised her head slightly and peeked out the windshield. Frances was walking toward the brown station wagon parked in her driveway. She was carrying a small leather handbag.

"Frances is getting into her car," Nancy reported to Bess. "She's starting the car . . . she's pulling out of the driveway . . . she's heading east on Montclair Drive. . . ." She sat up and turned on the ignition. "Okay, Bess, here we go. Now the fun part of surveillance begins."

"I'm ready," Bess declared. She reached into the pocket of her jeans jacket and whipped out a pair of dark glasses and a crumpled-up blue baseball cap. "My disguise," she announced, slipping them on.

For the next ten minutes, Nancy followed Frances, trying to keep a discreet distance behind her. When Frances pulled onto a busy boulevard leading to downtown River Heights, Nancy allowed a couple of cars to get between them.

"What are you doing that for, Nan?" Bess cried out. "You'll lose her!"

"Not if I can help it," Nancy said. "I just want to make sure she doesn't see us."

A few minutes later Frances pulled up to the drive-in window of the River Heights National Bank. Nancy parked in the bank's lot, reached into her glove compartment, and produced a pair of binoculars.

"Wow, you came prepared," Bess said admiringly.

Nancy grinned, then adjusted the focus on the binoculars. "Frances is at an automatic-teller cash machine," she told Bess. "She seems to be getting money out. Just a second." She started counting. ". . . Seventeen, eighteen, nineteen, twenty," she said after a moment. "Frances just withdrew twenty twenty-dollar bills. Now she's putting them in a white envelope and sticking the envelope in her purse."

"That's four hundred dollars!" Bess exclaimed.

"Yup," Nancy agreed, lowering her binoculars. "I wonder if that's how much she had when Yasmine saw the bundle of cash in her purse."

A minute later Frances's car was back on the busy boulevard, heading toward her home. Nancy and Bess followed.

Back on Montclair Drive, Nancy parked in the same spot. She watched as Frances stepped out of her station wagon and went inside.

Nancy checked her watch. "It's just before eleven. I guess we wait some more now," she told Bess.

Bess put her feet up on the dashboard and pushed her dark glasses up her nose. "So, Nan—what do you think that four hundred dollars is for? Do you think she's being blackmailed?"

Nancy shook her head. "Frances doesn't strike me as a killer," she admitted, leaning back in her seat. "Yasmine's con artist theory is starting to sound more likely—especially if Frances has been withdrawing four hundred dollars from the bank every Saturday and taking it someplace." She added, "I wish I knew more about Loretta. She seemed like such an odd character."

At eleven-thirty the girls saw Yasmine come out of her house, with her three dogs on their leashes. "She's following your instructions, Nan," Bess said, grinning. "She hasn't even glanced our way."

"Good," Nancy said. "If Frances happens to look out the window, Yasmine won't blow our cover."

At noon Frances walked out the door again. Nancy noticed that she paused on the front stoop, opened her purse, pulled the white envelope out of it, and nodded to herself.

"She's still got the money," Nancy said excitedly to Bess. "Maybe she's going to deliver it to someone now."

Frances got back into the station wagon. But this time, as the girls drove behind her, they weren't heading toward downtown but in a different direction altogether.

"Where's she going?" Bess said after they'd been on the road for a few minutes.

"I'm not sure," Nancy replied. They were driving into an older part of town, full of dingy stores, beauty parlors, diners, and run-down apartment buildings. The sidewalks were crowded with pedestrians.

Suddenly Nancy spotted something in her rearview mirror. Behind her was a gray sedan. And behind the gray sedan was a snazzy yellow convertible she knew she'd seen before.

"I think Craig Chandler is following us," she said uneasily to Bess. "Don't turn around. You should be able to see him in the mirror. He's two cars back."

"You're right," Bess said after a second, sounding amazed. "But, Nan, why would he do such a weird thing?"

"Good question," Nancy replied. "He could have been behind us all morning. I was so busy watching Frances, I didn't even notice. It never occurred to me that somebody would be tailing *us*."

Just then Frances turned the corner onto a quiet side street and pulled into a parking space. Nancy drove past her and parked farther down the block. Then she turned around to see Frances walking into a small pink storefront.

"Come on, Bess," Nancy said, getting out of the car. "Let's go see what Frances is up to."

When the girls reached the pink store, they saw a flickering neon sign in the large front window. It read:

MADAME DESTINY
FORTUNES TOLD
TAROT CARDS READ
ALL PROBLEMS SOLVED

Nancy couldn't see inside the window, which was covered with heavy orange curtains.

"That's it," Bess said, slapping her hands together. "We've solved the mystery. Frances isn't a murderer *or* the victim of a con artist. She gets a tarot card reading done every Saturday, and she's too embarrassed to tell anybody about it."

"A four-hundred-dollar tarot card reading?" Nancy looked skeptical. "That's pretty expensive. Come on, let's go back and wait in the car. I don't want her to see us here."

Back in the Mustang, Nancy glanced around and noticed that Craig was parked down the block from her. He was hiding his face behind a newspaper, although she could still see the top of his blond head. Nancy frowned. What was he up to?

Then Nancy noticed something even more peculiar. The gray sedan—the one she'd seen between her and Craig—was parked across the street from him. A red-haired man was sitting behind the wheel, also reading a newspaper.

What was going on? Nancy wondered, more confused than ever. Was the red-haired man following her—and Frances—too? But why? She was about to jot down his license plate number when Bess elbowed her.

"Nan!" she murmured. "Frances is leaving Madame Destiny's place!"

Nancy's head whipped around. Frances was just coming out.

Then an idea came to her. "I've got a plan, Bess," she said quickly. "But I need your help."

Within seconds Nancy was speed-walking down the sidewalk, wearing Bess's dark glasses and baseball cap. She had her face buried in her Mustang owner's manual. Her heart was thumping. Would she be able to pull off her plan?

Frances was standing by her station wagon, fumbling through her purse for her keys. Nancy was just a few feet away from her.

"Now!" Nancy told herself. She speeded up, and just as she passed Frances, she dropped her right arm casually to her side. Her elbow knocked Frances's purse out of her hands.

"Oh!" Frances cried out.

"I'm so sorry!" Nancy exclaimed in an innocent tone of voice. "Here, let me get that for you."

Springing forward, Nancy bent down and grabbed the elderly woman's fallen purse. She surreptitiously tilted it to spill its contents out on the sidewalk. Casting a quick eye over the pile— keys, wallet, balled-up tissues, a ballpoint pen, a tube of lipstick, a small plastic comb—Nancy stifled a gasp.

The white envelope wasn't there!

4

An Evil Omen

Nancy's hands deftly shuffled around the spilled contents of Frances's purse. No, the white envelope full of cash definitely wasn't there. Frances must have left the money inside Madame Destiny's shop, Nancy thought excitedly.

Frances's voice broke into her thoughts. "You!"

Nancy peeked up at Frances over the rim of her sunglasses. Frances was pointing a trembling finger at Nancy, her eyes flashing with anger.

"You're that Nancy girl. You were at my house last night!" Frances said accusingly.

"Mrs. Kittredge!" Nancy said, smiling brightly. "I didn't recognize you—how are you? I'm really sorry about bumping into you like that." She stuffed Frances's belongings back into her purse and handed it up to her.

Frances grabbed the purse and tucked it under her arm. "What are you doing here?" she asked angrily.

Nancy stood up and wiped her hands on her jeans. "I'm getting a reading done at Madame Destiny's," she replied, thinking quickly.

The expression in Frances's eyes changed instantly. Why did she look so alarmed all of a sudden? Nancy wondered. "You're . . . getting a reading?" Frances asked nervously.

"Sure—why not?" Nancy replied, trying to sound breezy and friendly. "And what brings you to this neighborhood, Mrs. Kittredge?"

But Frances turned away and rattled her car keys. "Excuse me," she muttered. "I have to hurry off. I'm late for an appointment." With that, she got into her car, slamming the door behind her.

Nancy waited, confused, on the sidewalk. Frances started her car with a roar, and a minute later she had disappeared down the street.

Bess had gotten out of the Mustang and was hurrying toward Nancy. "I think Frances recognized me when she drove past your car just now," she said breathlessly. "What happened, anyway?"

Nancy filled her in. "Frances got really scared when I told her I was going into Madame Destiny's," she said, frowning thoughtfully.

"And you know, I just remembered something. You remember that article on con artists I was talking about yesterday?"

"Sure," Bess replied.

"It also mentioned a pretty common con used by shady fortune-tellers," Nancy went on. "Apparently the fortune-tellers convince their clients that they're under a terrible curse. Then they offer to lift the curse in exchange for a lot of money."

"Hmm," Bess murmured. "Do you think Madame Destiny might be pulling this con on poor Frances?"

"I'm not sure," Nancy replied. "It's worth checking out, though, especially since Frances left the envelope full of money in Madame Destiny's shop."

Then Nancy remembered something. She quickly turned and glanced down the street.

The red-haired man in the gray sedan was gone now. Craig Chandler's yellow convertible, though, was still parked in its spot.

Nancy bit her lip, considering. She was eager to talk to Craig, but that would have to wait, she decided. "Why don't we go in and meet Madame Destiny?" she said to Bess, nodding toward the nearby storefront. "I'd like to get a reading done. I want to see if she says there's a curse on me."

"Just what you need—a curse," Bess remarked dryly.

The girls stepped inside Madame Destiny's shop. They found themselves in a small, dimly lit reception room. The walls were covered with colorful Indian-print cloths, and the furniture consisted of a desk, some folding chairs, and a cheap-looking coffee table. On the table dog-eared issues of a magazine titled *American Psychic* lay beside a vase of plastic flowers.

"What do we do now, Nan?" Bess whispered anxiously. "There's nobody here."

There was a door across the room marked Private. It creaked open just then, and a slender guy in his late twenties walked out. He was about five feet nine inches tall, wearing a baggy white shirt and black pants. He had curly brown hair and high cheekbones.

His catlike green eyes stared first at Bess, then at Nancy. "I am Dmitri," he said in a soft voice with a faint European accent. "May I help you ladies?"

"Yes," Nancy spoke up, taking off her dark glasses. "I'd like to get a reading done."

Dmitri clasped his hands together and nodded. "Madame is available. Please, come with me."

"Wait out here for me," Nancy said to Bess, then followed Dmitri through the door.

The inner room was even darker than the reception area. It was lit only by several large, dripping candles set on small tables in the room's corners. The air was filled with the heavy aroma of sandalwood incense.

Nancy blinked in the semidarkness. Dmitri stood in the middle of the room, next to a table covered with a linen cloth. Nancy could see a heavyset woman sitting behind it, dressed in a black hooded robe. There wasn't enough light to make out her features.

Nancy made her way over to the table, being careful not to trip over anything.

"Madame Destiny," Dmitri announced, bowing slightly.

"Dmitri, a candle," Madame Destiny called out in a dramatic voice, rolling her *r*'s with a flourish.

Dmitri took one of the large candles and set it down on the cloth-covered table. "Madame," Dmitri said with another bow, then left the room.

With the candle on the table, Nancy could see Madame Destiny much better now. Most of her face was covered by a black lace veil, except for her thickly charcoaled eyebrows and pale blue eyes. She had shoulder-length black hair with a dramatic white streak in it. Nancy guessed that the woman was in her fifties or sixties.

"Sit down, my dear," Madame Destiny told Nancy, waving her hand at a folding chair. Nancy saw that Madame's fingernails were extremely long and pointed and were painted a bright shade of purplish red.

Nancy obeyed. "I've never had a reading done before," she told her. She didn't add that she didn't believe in them.

"A novice," Madame Destiny murmured, nodding. "It is good that you have come to me. Through me, you will learn the secrets of happiness and success."

Madame Destiny spread her hands across the tabletop. In addition to the candle, the table held a crystal ball and a deck of tarot cards.

The fortune-teller picked up the cards. "Shuffle these for me, my dear," she commanded Nancy. "And concentrate with all your power."

Nancy looked puzzled. "Concentrate on what?"

"On whatever questions you have for the spirits, of course," Madame Destiny replied, arching one eyebrow. "They will communicate their answers to you through the tarot cards, which I will then interpret for you."

"I see," Nancy said, taking the deck from her.

After Nancy had shuffled, she handed the deck back to Madame Destiny. The fortune-teller closed her eyes and held the deck in her hands for a long moment. Then her eyes snapped open, and with a sharp flick of her wrist she slapped the top card of the deck down on the table.

On it was a picture of two intertwined arms. "This card tells me that you are very popular," Madame Destiny pronounced. "You draw friends to you like bees to a flower. You rise like a majestic rose in a field of lowly weeds, commanding attention!" She made a great sweeping gesture with her arm as she said this, almost knocking down her candle.

Nancy smiled and didn't say anything. She wanted Madame Destiny to say there was a curse on her, not offer her colorful flattery.

Madame Destiny turned over another card. "You are social, but you enjoy your solitude, too," she declared. "You are like a butterfly who must commune with other butterflies but then returns to her nest alone to contemplate her existence," she added importantly.

Madame Destiny continued to make similar pronouncements. Nancy noted that they were all vague general statements that could apply to just about anyone.

"You are logical, and yet you allow your emotions to guide you at times," Madame Destiny went on. "Your heart is like a forest, with its mighty green trees reaching toward the—What is it, Dmitri? You are disturbing my sacred communication with the spirits!"

Nancy whirled around in her seat. Dmitri had slipped silently into the room and was hovering near the door to the reception area. "I beg your pardon, Madame," he said quickly. "There's an important phone call for you. A, um, a client needs an immediate consultation. She says it's an emergency."

Madame Destiny hesitated for a second, then stood up. "Oh, very well," she said, sighing. "I am sorry, my friend. I'll be right back," she apologized to Nancy.

The fortune-teller swept through the doorway with a rustle of her black robe. Nancy sat at the table waiting for her, trying hard to see more details of the dark room. She didn't dare get up, since Dmitri still stood stiffly by the door.

Then Madame Destiny bustled back in. She made a curt gesture to Dmitri, and he left, shutting the door behind him.

The fortune-teller flounced down on her chair, her pale blue eyes not looking at Nancy. As she resumed Nancy's reading, Nancy noticed a marked change in her manner. She flipped over one card, then another, without uttering a word. Nancy wondered what had happened in the reception area.

"Did the spirits run out of things to say about me?" Nancy asked her with a grin.

Madame Destiny glared at her. "You shouldn't make light of the spirits," she warned in an icy voice. "They are very, very powerful."

Madame Destiny continued flipping cards. "I see that you are in some sort of investigation profession," she said after a moment. "Perhaps you are a police officer—or a private detective?"

Nancy's eyes widened. How did Madame Destiny know this? It definitely wasn't from the "spirits." Maybe the fortune-teller had recognized her from some article in the local newspaper, Nancy thought. But if so, why had she taken so long to bring it up?

Without waiting for Nancy's response, Madame Destiny turned over another card—and gasped.

On it was a picture of a skeleton holding a scythe, with a single word above it: Death.

5

Out of Control

Madame Destiny's hand fluttered dramatically to her heart. "This card can only mean one thing, my dear—a dark and terrible fate awaits you!"

Instead of being alarmed by these words, Nancy felt a tingle of excitement. Was she on the brink of solving the case? Was Madame Destiny going to follow up her dire prediction with an offer to take money from Nancy to pay off the "evil spirits"?

Nancy put on a worried look. "What kind of terrible fate?"

Madame Destiny closed her eyes and laid her hand on her forehead. Then she opened her eyes and said, "I see great danger from an unknown source."

"Oh, no!" Nancy moaned. "Madame Destiny—

is there anything I can do to keep it from happening? Anything at all?"

To Nancy's disappointment, Madame Destiny's reply had nothing to do with large sums of money. "Stay inside as much as possible for the next few weeks," she said. "Keep to yourself. The walls of your home will guard you from evil forces."

"Stay inside and keep to myself," Nancy repeated, puzzled. "That's it?"

Madame Destiny wiggled her finger disapprovingly. "Do not underestimate this very grave warning from the spirits," she murmured. "Your life is in peril. The Death card is the worst possible omen."

She pulled a red silk handkerchief from the sleeve of her cloak and wiped her brow. "The spirits have no more to say to you," she stated heavily. "Dmitri will take care of your bill."

Nancy didn't want to leave yet, but she didn't want to make Madame Destiny suspect her. She stood up, thanked her for the reading, and left the room.

Bess was sitting in the reception area, leafing through an issue of *American Psychic.* Dmitri was behind the desk, shuffling some papers.

Bess glanced up at Nancy and snapped the magazine shut. "All done?" she asked, staring at Nancy meaningfully.

Nancy nodded. "I just have to pay."

"That will be ten dollars," Dmitri said.

Nancy reached into her wallet and handed him the money. "Do you offer other services here besides tarot readings?" she asked him.

Dmitri's eyes narrowed as he looked at her. "Madame reads with her crystal ball as well," he replied after a moment. "And tea leaves. On rare occasions, she will do séances."

"Séances?" Bess repeated, her mouth dropping open. "You mean, like, talking to dead people?"

Dmitri nodded. "Yes, I suppose you could describe it that way. Madame is an expert at—"

"Dmitri! Have you finished with those documents?" Madame Destiny's stern voice rang out loudly from the inner room.

Flushing, Dmitri murmured, "Excuse me," and resumed going through the papers on his desk.

Once outside the shop, Bess turned to Nancy and said, "So what happened?"

"I'll tell you in a minute," Nancy said, holding up one hand. She saw that the yellow convertible was still parked down the block. "Come on. I want to have a talk with Craig first."

But as soon as Nancy and Bess started heading down the sidewalk, the convertible roared to life, made a U-turn, and sped away.

Nancy stopped in her tracks. "For someone who's not a suspect in this case, Craig's acting awfully suspicious," she remarked.

"If you want my opinion, everyone's acting suspicious," Bess piped up. "Wait till you hear about the phone call Madame Destiny got while you were in there with her."

Nancy grabbed Bess's arm eagerly. "What? You mean you heard the whole thing?"

Bess grinned mischievously. "I'll tell you all about it—but only over lunch, okay? I noticed this cute little diner around the corner. . . ."

"What'll you have?" the waitress asked Nancy and Bess, her head bent over a pad and pencil.

The girls were sitting in a quiet corner booth. It was just after one o'clock, but the diner was half empty.

"I'll have a pastrami on rye with mustard and a root beer float." Bess handed her menu to the waitress and flashed Nancy a smile. "Your turn."

"I'll have a hamburger and a lemonade," Nancy told the waitress. When the woman had gone away, Nancy leaned forward. "Well, Bess? What happened?"

Bess rolled up the sleeves of her pink sweatshirt. "While you were in with Madame Destiny, Dmitri and I were alone in the reception area," she began. "I tried to get him to talk, but he wasn't very friendly. Anyway," she went on, taking a deep breath, "the phone rang. Dmitri picked it up. Obviously, whoever was on the other end was pretty frantic."

"How could you tell?" Nancy asked her.

"Because Dmitri was saying these things," Bess explained, "like, 'Hold on a second, you know I can't interrupt her. What? Slow down, I can't understand you.'"

Nancy looked thoughtful. "Could you tell if it was a man or a woman?"

Bess shook her head. "He didn't call the person by name. Neither did Madame Destiny, when she came to the phone. What a creepy-looking woman, by the way," she added. "That hair and that black veil—and those mile-long red nails!"

The waitress returned and set the girls' drinks on the table, then wandered away again.

Bess tasted her root beer float. "Yum," she said happily. "So—Madame Destiny gets on the phone, and right away she's upset. Her eyes get huge, and she starts saying stuff like, 'You're kidding! Why, the nerve of that little— Well, I'll fix her right away.'" Bess added, "And she gave me a weird look, too."

"Dmitri told her that some client wanted an emergency consultation," Nancy said thoughtfully. "What you heard doesn't sound like that at all."

Bess leaned back in her seat. "That's all I have

to report. Now, tell me everything that happened while you were in with Madame Creepy.''

Nancy filled her in on the details of the reading. When she got to the part about Madame Destiny asking her if she was a detective, Bess's mouth dropped open. "So she *is* psychic!"

Nancy chuckled. "No way. More likely she's seen my picture in the papers." Her expression turned serious. "The point is, I'm not too thrilled that she might know who I am. She's probably suspicious of us now."

Bess frowned. "You're right—that's bad."

Nancy was silent for a minute. "Now that I think about it, I wonder if she was trying to give me a warning," she said finally.

Bess stirred her root beer float. "Huh?"

Nancy told her about the Death card. "She flipped over a bunch of cards, not saying anything. Then she came to the Death card and freaked out, told me I was in danger. It was like she was going through the deck, *looking* for that card, so she could scare me with it."

Bess dropped her spoon into her float. "But the Death card doesn't have anything to do with danger, Nancy!" she exclaimed. "It's a *good* card!"

Nancy's eyes widened. "What? How do you know this, Bess?"

"While I was waiting for you, I was checking out that magazine *American Psychic*," Bess explained excitedly. "There was an article in it about tarot cards. I was seeing what the different cards meant—it was kind of interesting. Anyway, I remember noticing the Death card, because it was so spooky-looking. But the article said it isn't spooky at all. It just means you're going to go through some big change in your life."

"Bess, that's fantastic detective work," Nancy told her, her blue eyes shining. "If what you say is true, Madame Destiny was definitely threatening me. Why else would she have lied about the meaning of that card?"

Bess made a face. "But why would she want to threaten you?"

Nancy took a sip of her lemonade. "Say that Madame Destiny was pulling an evil curse con on Frances. She wouldn't be too happy about having a detective show up at her shop. She'd want to get me off her trail somehow."

"So you think you're right about this evil curse business?" Bess asked her.

"I'm not sure yet," Nancy said. "But it kind of fits, doesn't it? We know Frances left four hundred dollars at Madame Destiny's today, and she may have done the same the other Saturdays, too. And she's been all jittery and weird since Jake's death. Thinking there's an evil curse hanging over your head would do that to you, don't you think?"

51

Bess nodded. "But how about Craig? How do you suppose he fits in?"

"I have no idea." Nancy looked troubled. "I'll have to find out more about him from Yasmine—as subtly as possible. He's her boyfriend, after all." She paused, then said, "And there's the red-haired guy in the gray sedan. Maybe it was a coincidence, but I think he was following us, too."

"And don't forget about Loretta," Bess threw in. "You were wondering about her, too."

"Right." Nancy sighed. "Plus, I still want to find out about Jake's death." She shook her head. "Boy, do we have a lot of work ahead of us!"

It was after three by the time Nancy got home. Her father and Hannah were both out. Dropping her car keys and purse on the front hall table, she headed for the kitchen. She swung herself up on the counter and picked up the phone. She requested the number for the Lake Sacandaga Village police force from the operator, then she dialed it.

"Police department," a male voice answered.

Nancy introduced herself, then said, "I was wondering whether I could get a copy of the report on Jake Kittredge's death. He died in a sailing accident at Lake Sacandaga in April of this year."

"Are you with the police?" the man asked.

"No," Nancy replied. "I'm a private investigator in River Heights, and I'm working on—"

The man cut her off. "Sorry. No can do, miss. We only issue copies of the report for official police business." With that, he hung up.

"Oh, great," Nancy muttered in frustration, then dialed another number. "I guess I'm going to have to bring Chief McGinnis in on this one." Nancy knew the River Heights police chief from various cases she'd helped his officers with.

Unfortunately, she learned that the chief was out of town until Monday morning. "Try him again then," the deputy she talked to advised her.

Hanging up, Nancy realized she would have to put off the matter of Jake's death for a couple of days.

She tried Yasmine next. An answering machine picked up. Nancy heard a recording of Yasmine's voice, sounding frantic and rushed, with one of her dogs barking in the background.

"Hi! Please leave a message for Naguib, Reema, or Yasmine Nasser at the tone—be quiet, Izzy!—and one of us will call you right back. You have thirty seconds to talk." Beep!

Oh, boy, one of those thirty-second deals, Nancy thought. She started talking very fast. "Yasmine, this is Nancy. Give me a call—I've got some information for you. If you miss me here, George, Bess, and I will be at the South of the

53

Border Café after six. Maybe you can join us there for dinner? Otherwise I'll try you again."

Nancy hung up, then pulled the phone book from a drawer. She flipped through the pages until she found the name Chandler, but there was no listing for a Craig Chandler.

Putting back the phone book, Nancy climbed down nimbly from the counter. "I guess I'll have to track down Craig through Yasmine," she thought.

Nancy went upstairs to jot down notes on the case while the details were still fresh in her mind. Then, at five-thirty, she showered, changed into a denim dress and cowboy boots, and headed out of the house. She planned to drive over to the Marvins' to pick up the cousins, then head out to the restaurant. She still hadn't heard from Yasmine.

But just as Nancy came out the front door, something caught her eye. It was Loretta Hart, standing on the sidewalk, with Ariel on a leash. Her back was turned, yet Nancy could see that she was stuffing something into the pocket of her coat.

Curious, Nancy started walking toward her. "Hi," she called out.

Loretta whirled around. "Oh, hey," she said, smiling nervously. "You were at the Kittredges' house last night, right?"

Nancy returned her smile. "You're kind of far from there, aren't you?"

"I needed the exercise," Loretta replied quickly.

Exercise? Nancy thought skeptically. The neighborhood Frances and Yasmine lived in was almost five miles away. And Loretta was wearing high heels—hardly the shoes for a ten-mile walk. Out loud, Nancy said, "It's a nice evening for it."

"Yeah, sure," Loretta drawled vaguely. She glanced down at Ariel, who was sniffing some plants. "Well, the dog's getting kinda antsy— guess I'd better go." Without waiting for Nancy's reply, she started down the sidewalk.

Now, what was all that about? Nancy wondered as she headed back to her Mustang. Loretta was definitely acting suspicious.

Ten minutes later, when Nancy pulled up in front of the Marvins' house, she found Bess and George sitting on the doorstep, waiting. As soon as they hopped in the car, George said, "Well, thanks for solving the mystery without me, Drew! Bess told me all about your big day."

Nancy raised her eyebrows at Bess, who was getting into the backseat. "You told her we solved the mystery?"

Bess flipped her hair over her shoulders and said, "Well, I *did* tell her all about my brilliant research on tarot cards."

Nancy chuckled as she shifted gears and re-sumed driving. "Don't worry, George. There's plenty of mystery solving left to do," she said, then proceeded to fill her in. She finished by telling both cousins about her brief encounter with Loretta.

"What do you think she was up to?" George asked.

"I'm not sure," Nancy replied. "It's hard to believe she was out on such a long walk."

The girls fell silent as they reached downtown River Heights. The South of the Border Café was on Lafayette Street, a strip of trendy boutiques and restaurants. As Nancy turned onto it, she could see that the sidewalks were mobbed with people.

George groaned. "The place we're going to doesn't take reservations, and it looks like there are about a million people out tonight."

"I think the restaurant's just past this intersec-tion," Nancy said, putting her foot on the brake as the light turned yellow. "I've never been there, but——"

She stopped as she realized that something was very wrong. The car wasn't slowing down.

Startled, Nancy pumped the brake harder. But the car still didn't respond. They were cruising down the busy street at forty miles per hour, rolling right into the intersection.

George clutched the dashboard. "Nan, that light just turned red!"

"I know," Nancy replied tersely. "My brakes don't seem to be working."

"What?" Bess cried out.

Luckily, there were no cars in front of her, but Nancy saw the drivers on the cross street begin to accelerate for their green light. And dozens of unsuspecting pedestrians were stepping out into the crosswalk.

In a matter of seconds, the Mustang would plow right into them!

6

Sabotage

"We're going to die!" Bess screamed, covering her eyes.

"Not if I can help it," Nancy said fiercely.

She jammed her left hand down on the car horn. Hearing the horn blare, the pedestrians in the crosswalk looked up and began dashing for the curb. At the same time, Nancy used her right hand to downshift to second gear. The Mustang shuddered, sputtered, and lost speed.

Then Nancy grabbed the emergency brake and pulled—hard. The Mustang lurched violently, then ground to a halt halfway into the intersection.

Nancy closed her eyes and took a deep breath.

Bess peeked through her fingers. "Hey, we're still alive," she said in amazement.

"You crazy teenagers! Learn how to drive!"

Nancy opened her eyes and glanced out the window. A number of cars were backed up on the cross street, and a middle-aged man in a silver sedan was leaning out and yelling at her. Other drivers were casting angry looks in her direction.

"Oh, boy," Nancy muttered, then switched on her flashers. "Bess and George, can you go find a traffic cop to help out with this mess? I have to call a garage."

"Sure thing, Nan," George replied shakily.

As Nancy got out of the car and headed for a phone booth, she noticed a big crowd gathered at the intersection. "Huge pile-up," she heard some guy say to a girl. "I saw them take away a bunch of people in an ambulance."

Nancy chuckled nervously. The guy was obviously lying to impress the girl, and yet he was eerily close to the truth. A few seconds more, and a lot of people would have been hurt—or worse.

Nancy called the nearest garage—Mabel Rose's on Main Street—and headed back to the car. By then, two cops had arrived and were directing traffic. Bess and George were leaning against the Mustang, looking unhappy.

"You the owner of this vehicle?" one of the cops, a stocky young man, called out to Nancy. "I'm going to need to take a report."

Nancy told him what had happened. "My brakes were fine until we got here," she finished. "Between my house and here I must have stopped or slowed down half a dozen times, and there wasn't any problem. I have no idea what went wrong."

A tow truck pulled up just then. A short woman in her forties got out. She was dressed in grease-covered jeans and a flannel shirt.

She walked up to the Mustang, lifted the hood, and peeked in. "Uh-huh," she said thoughtfully. Then she got down on the ground and slid under the car. "Uh-huh," she repeated after a moment.

Nancy went up to her. "Are you Mabel Rose?" she said, bending down. "I'm Nancy Drew. I talked to you on the phone."

The woman slid out from under the car and stood up. She rubbed her hands together. "Mabel Rose Dougherty," she said crisply. "I'm going to tow this baby back to my garage. Right off the bat, I'd venture you have a loose bleed valve."

"A loose bleed valve?" Nancy repeated, puzzled. "But I thought it was my brakes."

"When your bleed valve's loose, you lose brake fluid every time you put your foot on the brake pedal," Mabel Rose explained patiently. "So each time you braked this evening, you lost a little fluid. By the time you got to this intersection, you had no fluid left at all."

Nancy frowned. "How do bleed valves get loose?"

Mabel Rose shrugged. "Sometimes it just happens—freak of nature, accident, bad luck, whatever. But more likely than not, some joker with a crescent wrench and a little automobile know-how spent a few minutes under your car and—*rrrip!*" She made a violent tearing motion with her hands.

"You mean somebody sabotaged Nancy's car?" Bess spoke up in a trembling voice.

Nancy fell silent as the weight of Mabel Rose's disturbing statement sunk in. Someone may have tried to kill her—but who? A lot of people could have tampered with her car that afternoon: Craig, Madame Destiny, Dmitri, even Loretta.

Mabel Rose's voice interrupted her thoughts. "I'll try to have your car fixed up for you in a few hours," she was saying to Nancy.

"Great," Nancy said. "We were planning to eat at the South of the Border Café. I'll call you around eight or nine, if that's okay with you."

After exchanging a few words with the traffic cops, Nancy, Bess, and George headed down the street to the restaurant.

"Someone really wants you off this case, Nan," Bess said anxiously as they went inside.

"I know it," Nancy replied grimly. "But I can't drop the case now. I'll just have to be extra careful, that's all." Bess and George exchanged a worried look but said nothing. They were used to Nancy's unflinching determination when it came to solving mysteries.

The girls checked their coats and went into the

61

busy dining room. The decor was Southwestern: cream-colored adobe walls, colorful hanging tapestries, and huge cactus plants in terra-cotta pots. Nancy could barely hear the live guitar music above the noise of voices and clattering plates.

The girls stood in a line of people waiting to be seated. "Do you see the maître d'?" George asked Nancy, bewildered.

Before she could reply, Nancy felt an energetic tap on her shoulder. She turned around to see Yasmine's grinning face.

"Hey!" Nancy said happily. "You made it!"

"Hi, Yasmine," Bess piped up. "Hope you're not too hungry. I think we're in for a major wait."

Yasmine glanced around. "Hang on a second," she said, then wandered off.

She came back a minute later. "I got us a table. Come on, guys."

"How'd you manage that?" George asked, amazed.

"The maître d' is a friend of Craig's," Yasmine whispered.

A slim man with slicked-back hair seated them. "Enjoy your dinner," he said, handing them menus. "Say hi to Craig," he added to Yasmine.

"I will," Yasmine replied. "Thanks, Hector."

Nancy leaned forward. "Craig mentioned that he worked in the restaurant business. Is that how he knows Hector?"

Yasmine nodded. "Hector was a waiter at Sperry's before he came here."

"Sperry's?" George repeated. "That's the place on Cornell Avenue, right?"

"Does Craig own it?" Nancy asked Yasmine.

"Own it?" Yasmine gave her a funny smile. "No, he's a waiter there. He's working there tonight and tomorrow morning, in fact."

A waiter? Nancy thought to herself. How could he afford his fancy yellow convertible on a waiter's salary? And why hadn't he said he was a waiter when she asked him what he did?

"So, Nancy, I'm dying to know what you guys found out today," Yasmine said, putting her menu down. "You left me a message that you had some information."

"Right," Nancy said. Putting Craig out of her mind, she filled Yasmine in on the day's events— everything from following Frances to Madame Destiny's to the failed brakes.

As Nancy talked, she didn't mention that Craig apparently had trailed her to Madame Destiny's, then took off when she went to talk to him about it. She felt uncomfortable suspecting him—after all, Yasmine was her friend. Besides, she didn't want to say anything until she had some solid evidence against Craig—if there was any.

Yasmine went pale as Nancy finished telling her story. "Someone tampered with your brakes?" she gasped. "Nancy, this is crazy. When I asked you to check on Frances, I didn't mean for you to put yourself in any danger. If anything happened to you, I'd never forgive myself."

Nancy touched Yasmine's arm. "It's okay," she reassured her. "It's not the first time someone's tried to scare me off a case. So don't even try to talk me into dropping this investigation, okay?"

"Okay," Yasmine agreed, looking doubtful.

The waiter came by just then to drop off some chips and salsa and take their orders. When he'd gone away, Yasmine said, "So you think Frances might be getting conned by this fortune-teller? I could believe that—she's pretty superstitious."

"What do you mean?" George asked, munching on a chip.

"She's always been afraid of black cats, walking under ladders, stuff like that," Yasmine explained. "And she reads her horoscope in the paper every morning."

"Really?" Nancy said with interest. If Frances was that superstitious, she thought, Madame Destiny could easily con her with an "evil spell."

"Couldn't we just *ask* Frances if she's paying Madame Destiny to get rid of some evil curse?" Bess suggested. "I mean, that would be the easiest thing, wouldn't it?"

The waiter brought the girls' drinks, four frozen pineapple-and-coconut shakes. Nancy took a sip of hers, then said, "If Madame Destiny really is a con artist, she would probably have warned Frances to keep the whole thing a secret, or else the power of the evil curse would be tripled."

The girls kept discussing the case over their dinner of grilled chicken with bitter chocolate sauce and seafood tacos. At eight-thirty, Nancy excused herself and called Mabel Rose's.

"I'm done fixing up your car," Mabel Rose told her. "It was the bleed valve all right, just like I said. You're lucky you weren't doing fifty-five on the highway when your brake fluid ran out."

Hanging up, Nancy thought again about the people who'd had the opportunity that day to tamper with her car. If Madame Destiny was indeed conning Frances, she—and her assistant, Dmitri—would have had the strongest motives. But Nancy still had a lot of unanswered questions about Craig and Loretta, too.

When Nancy walked in her front door that night, the phone was ringing. Neither Carson nor Hannah was home, so she rushed to the kitchen to answer it. "Hello?"

"Is this Nancy?" a woman's voice said softly. "It's Edwina Leidig. I'm sorry to call so late."

"That's okay," Nancy said. "Did you want to speak to my dad? I think he's out."

"Actually, I wanted to speak to you," Edwina cut in. "After you left yesterday, I suddenly remembered Carson's mentioning that you were a detective. And I got to thinking, why not hire you to help me find that scoundrel Thomas Whittle? The police haven't done much so far—I'm sure they're too busy chasing murderers and bank robbers to help out an old lady like me."

"I'd love to track down Thomas Whittle for you, Edwina," Nancy replied. "But I'm in the middle of a case right now. Maybe after I'm through with it?"

"Oh, that'd be fine," Edwina said gratefully. "Whenever you're ready, you come by and see me."

They talked for a few more minutes, then said goodbye. Just as Nancy was leaving the kitchen, the phone began ringing again. Edwina must have forgotten to tell her something, Nancy thought.

She turned and picked up the phone. "Hello?"

There was a crackly silence. "Hello?" Nancy repeated. "Edwina, is that you?"

"Listen carefully, Nancy Drew," an unfamiliar voice said in a chilling whisper. "What happened to you today—you won't be so lucky the next time. Do I make myself clear?"

7

A Magic Brew

"Who is this?" Nancy demanded.

There was a click, then a long tone. The threatening caller had hung up.

Nancy put the receiver down slowly. She closed her eyes and repeated the brief message in her mind, trying to identify the voice. But the person had deliberately spoken in a low, breathy whisper, and she couldn't even tell if it had been a man or a woman.

"At least I know for sure now that the loose bleed valve wasn't an accident," she said to herself. Someone was serious about wanting her off the case. And whoever it was clearly was watching her; he or she knew that Nancy had survived the brake failure tonight.

Nancy shivered and checked the door locks

before she went upstairs to get ready for bed. "Stay calm, Drew," she told herself sternly. "Don't let this creep scare you."

But as she climbed the stairs, she found herself hoping that either her father or Hannah would get home soon.

In the morning light, Nancy felt better. Driving to Frances's house with Bess and George, she was more determined than ever to solve the case.

"I don't understand why we have to follow Frances two days in a row," Bess grumbled.

Nancy turned onto Montclair Drive. "We're not following Frances today," she told her. "We're paying Loretta a visit while Frances is out."

"How do you know Frances won't be there, Nan?" George piped up from the backseat.

"I phoned Yasmine, and she said Frances goes to church on Sunday mornings," Nancy said.

"What excuse are you going to give for our being there?" Bess asked.

"Don't worry." Nancy chuckled. "I'll think of something by the time we get there."

When Nancy rang Frances's doorbell, Loretta answered, dressed in a powder blue silk robe. "Hey," she said, her dark eyes darting from Nancy to Bess to George. "If you all are here to see Frances, she isn't home."

"Oh, that's all right," Nancy said cheerfully. "Bess decided that she might want to get a Chinese crested herself, and she wanted to take another look at Ariel."

Bess shot Nancy an indignant "why me?" look. Then she turned to Loretta and smiled weakly. "That's right," she said, playing along. "I thought Ariel was a really, um, *terrific* dog, and I wondered if I could spend a few minutes with her."

Loretta frowned, as if she were mulling it over. Then she said, "I guess that would be okay. Come on in. The place is kind of a mess, though."

Nancy, George, and Bess followed her to the den. "You all want some coffee?" Loretta offered.

"I'd love some," Nancy replied, and George and Bess nodded.

Loretta disappeared into the hallway, returning a few minutes later with a tray. She handed each of the girls a cup, then said, "Here's milk and sugar. Help yourselves."

Nancy studied her cup, which had an I Love Texas logo on it. "Texas—is that where you're from, Loretta?"

"Oh, I'm from all over," Loretta answered vaguely. "Frances got that old mug when she and Jake went to Houston a few years ago." She looked around distractedly. "Where's that dog? Ariel!"

69

Nancy noticed an enormous sapphire ring on Loretta's right hand. She sure likes nice clothes and jewelry, Nancy thought. Out loud she said, "That's a beautiful ring, Loretta."

Loretta glanced at it quickly. "Oh, this old thing. Well, thanks."

A minute later Ariel came bounding into the room. "She's all yours," Loretta told Bess.

Bess reached over to pet her. "Hi, Ariel," she said halfheartedly. Ariel bared her teeth and growled at Bess. "Oh!" Bess cried out.

"Bess is a little jumpy," George told Loretta.

"The three of us almost had a really bad car accident last night," Nancy added, watching the housekeeper's reaction carefully.

Loretta's dark eyes flashed. Nancy could have sworn that for a second she looked afraid.

"That's too bad," Loretta murmured. "You all weren't hurt, were you?"

Nancy took a sip of coffee. "No, but we almost were," she said. She gave Loretta a detailed account of the incident. "It was the strangest thing. The mechanic had no idea how the bleed valve came loose."

"Cars can be weird," Loretta said vaguely, then set her coffee cup down on the table. "Listen, if you all are finished with the dog, I'd better get started on my day."

The girls rose. "Well, thanks for letting us see Ariel," Nancy said, elbowing Bess. "Right?"

"Right!" Bess exclaimed. "'Bye, Ariel. If I'm, um, lucky, I'll get a dog just like you real soon."

When they were back in the Mustang, Nancy said, "I thought Loretta acted fishy when I brought up the bleed valve thing."

"I noticed it, too," George spoke up. "Do you think she could have done it?"

"It's possible," Nancy replied, starting the car. "But why? That's the big question."

Ten minutes later Nancy pulled up in front of Sperry's Restaurant on Cornell Avenue. "Hope you guys are hungry," she said brightly. "We're having Sunday brunch—my treat."

"Brunch, my foot," George said, grinning. "You're here to grill Craig Chandler, right?"

Nancy chuckled. "I can't fool you."

The inside of Sperry's was dark and wood-paneled. The hostess seated them in a booth, which was lit by a chrome Art Deco sconce.

The girls scanned the menu. "Mmm, Belgian waffles with blueberry-raspberry sauce," Bess said.

Craig came up to them just then, pad in hand. "Are you ready to order?" he asked in a crisp, professional voice. "Or do you need a few—"

He stopped when he recognized the girls. His smile faded. "Oh, hi," he said uncertainly. "What are you guys doing here?"

"Having brunch," Nancy declared. "How are you, Craig?"

71

"Okay," he replied nervously. He fixed his eyes on his pad and held his pencil poised above it. "Can I take your orders?"

He's definitely not happy to see us, Nancy thought. "I'll have the apricot-cinnamon French toast and a glass of orange juice," she said.

After the cousins had ordered, Craig grabbed all the menus and turned to go.

"You know, Craig, I could have sworn I saw you driving around yesterday," Nancy said. "Around noon, I think it was."

Craig stopped and glanced at her over his shoulder. "Er, you must be mistaken," he replied awkwardly. "I was here all day." Then he hurried off to the kitchen.

Bess leaned across the table. "Did he put his personality in the deep freeze, or what?"

"He seemed so nice when we met him on Friday," George added.

Nancy looked thoughtful. "He's lying through his teeth is what he's doing," she said. "We saw him, Bess. But why is he trying to cover it up?"

When Craig brought their food, Nancy decided to try the same tack she'd used with Loretta. "So, Craig, you wouldn't believe what happened to us last night."

Craig set their plates down. "What?"

Nancy told him about the failed brakes, watching him carefully the whole time. Craig seemed genuinely concerned. "Wow, you guys were

72

lucky," he said sympathetically. "You could really have been hurt."

When he'd gone away, Nancy frowned. "If he's the one who tampered with the bleed valve, he's a fantastic actor. He seemed really surprised to hear what happened."

Forty-five minutes later the girls got back in the Mustang. Craig had been a little friendlier when they'd paid their check, but not much.

"So what do we do now?" George asked Nancy.

Nancy started the car. "We're going to Madame Destiny's. Maybe we'll find some answers there."

But a surprise awaited Nancy when she turned onto Madame Destiny's street. The gray sedan from the day before was parked across from her shop. The red-haired man was in it. As before, he had a newspaper half covering his face.

Nancy drove past him, turned the corner, and parked on a cross street. She turned to George. "Listen, I want you to do something for me. There's a gray sedan across from Madame Destiny's shop, with a red-haired man inside."

"The guy you thought was following us yesterday!" Bess piped up.

Nancy nodded. "Maybe he works for Madame Destiny, as a follow-up guy for the evil curse scam. George, he hasn't ever seen you. Could you walk over and start talking to him—maybe ask for directions? See what you can learn about him."

"Sure thing." George jumped out of the car.

Nancy then turned to Bess. "You stay here and keep an eye on the car. I'm going to pay Madame Destiny a visit. I'll be back in fifteen minutes."

Bess pulled a fashion magazine out of her purse. "Lucky for me I brought reading material," she said, leaning back in her seat.

As Nancy walked briskly down Madame Destiny's street, she saw George leaning against the gray sedan, talking animatedly with the red-haired man. He was holding a large map and pointing a finger at it. Nancy slipped a piece of paper out of her purse and jotted down his license plate number.

When Nancy reached the fortune-teller's shop, she was glad to find that it was open on Sundays. She took a deep breath and went inside. Dmitri sat at the desk, leafing through a spiral-bound notebook.

Seeing Nancy, he snapped the notebook shut and rose to his feet. He smiled and bowed his head. "Welcome," he said pleasantly. "Nice to see you again. You would like another reading?"

Nancy wrung her hands together. "Yes, and it's very urgent," she said in a low, anxious voice. "Could I see Madame Destiny right away?"

Dmitri raised one eyebrow. "Certainly," he said. "Come with me, please."

Nancy followed Dmitri through the door to the inner room. Madame Destiny was lighting a tall black candle on her table. When she saw Nancy, she said, "Ah, you have come back. But did I not tell you yesterday to stay in your house?"

"And I should have listened to you, Madame," Nancy declared, rushing up to the table and sitting down. "Something terrible happened to me last night, just as you predicted!"

Sounding as distraught as possible, Nancy told the fortune-teller about her near accident. She tried to read the expression in the older woman's eyes as she talked, but they remained blank.

When Nancy had finished, Madame Destiny said sharply, "I saw this coming. Did I not warn you to take the spirits seriously?"

"Yes, yes, you did," Nancy said in a shaky voice. "And now I'm afraid, even in my own house. Isn't there anything I can do?"

Madame Destiny narrowed her eyes and stood up. "Wait here," she said. She swept off into a back room.

A few minutes later she reappeared, holding a tarnished silver goblet with a silver cobra carved around the stem. "Drink this," she told Nancy.

Nancy looked inside the goblet. It held a scarlet-colored liquid with a tangy, bitter smell —not appetizing in the least.

"What is it?" Nancy asked, making a face.

"A very special tea," Madame Destiny replied

in a hushed voice. "It will ward off the evil that hangs over your head like a dark storm cloud." She pushed the goblet toward Nancy's lips. "Drink it, my dear. Drink it before it's too late!"

Nancy hesitated. She didn't like to drink anything without knowing what it was. But if she didn't, Madame Destiny might get suspicious.

As Nancy pretended to take a sip, Madame Destiny tipped the goblet forward, forcing some tea into Nancy's mouth. "You must drink it *all*," the fortune-teller told her sternly.

Nancy coughed and turned her face away. A little bit of the tea had gone down her throat, leaving a taste like old leaves and grass cuttings. "I—I feel much better now," Nancy gasped. "Thank you." She stood up abruptly and left the room before Madame Destiny could make her drink more.

When Nancy got back to the Mustang, George and Bess were waiting. "Did you find out anything, Nan?" Bess called out the window.

Nancy slipped into the car. "Nothing much," she told her friends. "Madame Destiny makes awful tea, that's all. What about you, George? Did you find out anything about that red-haired man?"

"Sorry," George said, shrugging. "Nothing he said told me who he is or what he's doing there. And there's nothing revealing in his car, just a newspaper and a couple of old coffee cups.

But I did notice a red-and-white sticker on his windshield—it said 'Dependable.' Isn't there a company called Dependable Car Rental?"

"Of course," Nancy said, smiling. "Good work, George." Then her smile faded into a frown. "Except now we won't be able to trace his license plate number. I'm sure Dependable won't release the names of its customers."

George groaned. "Well, what next, Nan?"

"Home," Nancy said, starting up the car. "I need to do some thinking. I'll drop you guys off, and maybe we can regroup later."

By one o'clock, Nancy was sitting cross-legged on her bedroom floor, rereading the article about con artists. She noted with interest that con artists preferred working alone or in pairs, to limit the possibility of getting caught. "If that's true, maybe the red-haired man doesn't work for Madame Destiny. She's already got Dmitri working with her," Nancy said to herself.

Just then she felt a sharp pain in her stomach —the second or third pain in the past few minutes. With a sigh of impatience, she stood up and went downstairs to get something for it.

Hannah was in the kitchen making bread. The air was filled with the warm smell of baking.

"Hi, Nancy," Hannah called out. "I'm trying my hand at some new recipes. Be my guinea pig and taste this." She paused and frowned. "You're white as a sheet. Are you sick?"

Nancy leaned against the counter. A wave of dizziness washed over her, and her cheeks felt clammy and hot. "I thought it was just a stomachache," she answered, "but now . . ."

Just then a searing pain shot through her midsection. "Ouch!" she cried out.

Hannah laid a gentle hand on Nancy's shoulder. "Nancy, what's the matter?"

In reply, Nancy groaned loudly and sank to the floor.

8

Clues in the Dark

Carson came running into the kitchen. "What's going on?" His eyes swept anxiously over his daughter, who was doubled up on the floor. "Nancy, what's wrong?"

"It's my stomach," Nancy whispered through clenched teeth. "It hurts. A lot."

Hannah, who was kneeling beside her, glanced up at Carson. "Maybe we should call Dr. Arnstein."

"His number's in my study," Carson said. "I'll be right back. Hang tight, Nancy honey."

Dr. Arnstein lived just around the corner, and he was at the house in five minutes flat.

"Thanks so much for coming by on a Sunday, Doctor," Carson said gratefully.

"No problem," Dr. Arnstein replied.

After examining Nancy and asking her a number of questions, the doctor announced that she was suffering from food poisoning.

"Food poisoning!" Hannah said, alarmed. "I hope it's not from anything I made!"

"Nancy told me what she had to eat and drink today," Dr. Arnstein replied. "Any one of those things could have caused these symptoms."

He gave Nancy a medicine to calm her stomach and left her with strict instructions to stay in bed the rest of the day.

"You won't get any argument from me," Nancy said with a weak smile. "Sleep sounds like a great idea right now."

When Nancy woke up, her room was pitch-black. Her body was covered with a fine layer of sweat, and her hair clung damply to her face. She sat up, feeling disoriented. What time was it? What was she doing in bed? And then she remembered.

She reached over and clicked on her bedside light. Her alarm clock read six-thirty.

She picked up the phone and punched in Bess's number. "Hi, it's me," she said when Bess answered. "Are you feeling okay?"

"Huh?" Bess sounded confused. "Sure I'm feeling okay. Are you feeling okay?"

"No," Nancy replied. "That's why I'm asking. I think one of our suspects tried to poison me."

"What!" Bess shrieked.

Nancy explained what had happened to her earlier. "The way I figure it, three people had a chance to slip me something today," she said. Still feeling groggy, she squeezed her eyes shut to concentrate. "First, Loretta gave us some coffee. Then we had brunch at Sperry's, served to us by Craig. Then I had that awful tea at Madame Destiny's. I only took a little sip, but still . . ."

"It must have been the tea," Bess declared. "George and I had the coffee and brunch, too, and we're totally fine. George is in the den with my dad, watching some boring football game." She added dryly, "The way she's rooting and stomping her feet, I'm sure she's healthy."

Nancy chewed her lip, thinking. "No, it still could have been the coffee or the brunch. Loretta or Craig could have put something into my stuff and left yours and George's alone."

"That's true," Bess agreed.

Cradling the phone under her chin, Nancy swung her legs over the side of the bed and stood up slowly. She still felt lightheaded, but her stomach pains were gone.

"Can you guys come out with me for a while?" she said to Bess, reaching for her clothes. "I'd like to pay our suspects another round of visits. One of them will be very surprised to see me up and around, and I want to know which one."

"You want to go out and catch crooks in your condition?" Bess said.

81

"I'm fine," Nancy reassured her. "Really. I'll pick you guys up in fifteen minutes, okay?"

Nancy decided to drop in on Craig first. Just as she turned her car onto Cornell Avenue, she saw his yellow convertible pulling away from Sperry's parking lot.

"Lucky for us he put in a long day," Nancy said to George and Bess. "If he'd gone home earlier, we'd have missed him. And I have no idea where he lives."

Nancy followed Craig for three miles or so, always keeping one or two cars between them so he wouldn't spot her. After a while the yellow convertible zipped into the driveway of a shabby brick duplex. A second later Craig got out of his car and went inside the house. Nancy parked across the street.

"Do you have a plan, Nancy?" Bess whispered as they walked up to his door. "Am I going to have to pretend to love another mean little dog, or anything like that?"

Nancy chuckled. "No, nothing like that. This time I think a direct approach might be best."

Craig opened the door after Nancy had pressed the buzzer four times. His steel gray eyes widened when he saw the girls. "What are you doing here? How did you—" He paused and drew his mouth into a tense line. "You followed me, didn't you?"

"Just like you followed us yesterday, Craig," Nancy replied smoothly. "May we come in?"

"I'm busy," Craig replied curtly, starting to shut the door.

Nancy thrust her hand in the doorway, holding it open. She gazed at Craig levelly. "I'd like to know why you tried to poison me this morning."

"Poison you?" Craig spat out. "What are you talking about?"

"I'd also like to know why you tampered with my bleed valve," Nancy went on. "And why you tailed us to Madame Destiny's."

Craig stared at her for a moment, then shook his head. "You'd better come in," he said with a heavy sigh. "I can see we need to have a talk. This thing is really getting out of hand."

He led the girls into his living room. The only furniture in it was a tattered plaid sofa and love seat and a couple of TV trays. A tiger cat with one ear missing was sleeping on the orange shag rug.

"Please sit down," Craig said wearily. "Can I get anyone anything? Tea? Seltzer?"

"Nothing, thanks," Nancy said, and George and Bess shook their heads.

Craig plopped down on one end of the sofa. "Okay, I admit I was following you yesterday," he said after a moment. "You see, I wanted to solve this Frances Kittredge thing myself."

Nancy remembered his odd reaction on Friday,

when Yasmine told him that Nancy was going to be handling the case. "Go on," she urged him.

Craig folded his hands together and rested his chin on them. "Yasmine and I have been dating for four months now. We met at the animal shelter. At first I had no idea why she agreed to go out with me. I still don't, really."

He paused and smiled sadly. "She's sweet, she's smart, she's beautiful, and her family is loaded. What do I have to offer her? I'm a waiter. I never went to college. I live in a dump."

"You drive a pretty nice car," Nancy noted.

"It's not mine," Craig explained. "I'm leasing it. You see, that's the thing—I'm spending what little money I have trying to impress Yasmine. The car, the nice clothes, fancy places to eat. I put in double shifts at Sperry's this weekend just to try to keep up."

"Does she know you're doing this?" George asked gently.

Craig scowled. "No way. I'd never tell her."

Bess leaned forward. "And that's why you wanted to solve the Frances mystery yourself? So you could impress Yasmine?" She turned to Nancy and beamed. "Isn't that romantic?"

"It's pretty desperate is what it is," Craig muttered. "I thought if I followed you around, Nancy, I could get a jump on the case." He stared at the floor. "I feel like a first-class idiot."

"So you had nothing to do with the bleed

valve?'' Nancy asked again. "And you didn't try
to poison me this morning?''

Craig's head shot up. "Absolutely not,'' he said
firmly.

Nancy looked him in the eye. She couldn't be
completely sure, but the guy seemed to be telling
the truth.

"Okay, Craig,'' Nancy said finally. "Thanks for
leveling with us.''

Craig's face relaxed. "Thanks for giving me a
break, Nancy. I know I've been a real jerk.''

"You should give yourself a break, Craig,''
Nancy replied. "If you want my opinion, you
should stop worrying about impressing Yasmine.''

"Yeah, that's right,'' Bess put in. "Anyone can
see she's head over heels in love with—'' Then
her hands flew to her lips. "Oops! Should I have
said that? Do I have a big mouth, or what?''

After leaving Craig, the girls headed for
Frances's house to see Loretta. "One suspect
down, three to go—or is it four?'' George
quipped. "I've lost count.''

"Don't rule out Craig just yet,'' Nancy told her,
tossing her reddish blond hair.

"But, Nan!'' Bess protested. "It's obvious Craig
has nothing to do with ripping Frances off or
trying to hurt you. The only thing he's guilty of is
being nuts about Yasmine.'' She added dreamily,
"It's just like something out of the movies. Poor
guy falls in love with rich girl . . .''

"You're an incurable romantic, Bess," Nancy teased her.

They turned onto Montclair Drive and drove up to Frances's house. It was completely dark. "No one's home, I guess," Nancy said. She peered at her dashboard clock. "Eight-ten. Hmm . . . I guess we'll have to skip Loretta and head over to Madame Destiny's."

Just then she spotted Yasmine coming out the front door of her house, dressed in jeans and a baggy red sweater. Spotting the girls, Yasmine ran up to their car. "Are you here to see Frances?" she asked.

"Loretta, actually," Nancy replied, "but she's not here. Now we're going to Madame Destiny's."

Yasmine's eyes lit up. "Can I come with you? Maybe I could help out. I'm kind of getting lonely," she admitted, glancing over her shoulder at her big house. "Craig's been so busy, and my parents aren't coming home until Friday."

"Sure, why not?" Nancy said with a grin. "Jump in."

As they drove, Nancy filled Yasmine in on her day. She skipped over the details having to do with Craig: the brunch at Sperry's, the visit to his apartment. She also tried to downplay her bout of food poisoning.

"For all I know, it was something I had for breakfast," Nancy said lightly. "But it could also have been the coffee Loretta gave me, or the tea I had at Madame Destiny's."

Yasmine sighed. "If I'd known this case was going to get so dangerous, I would never have brought it up, Nancy."

"It's good you did," Nancy replied. "You're doing Frances a huge favor. And besides, I have a feeling we're getting close to a solution."

When Nancy reached Madame Destiny's street, she saw that it was eerily deserted. Dead leaves drifted along the sidewalk, buffeted by the wind, and a single streetlamp cast a dim yellow glow.

Nancy parked the car around the corner, then she and the girls went up to Madame Destiny's shop. The windows were dark, and a Closed sign hung on the door.

Nancy rapped on the door. "Hello?" she called. There was no answer.

On an impulse, Nancy reached down and turned the doorknob. To her surprise, it wasn't locked.

She opened the door and peeked inside. The reception area was dark and empty. "Hello!" she called out again. "Anybody in there?"

When there was no reply, Nancy turned to her friends. "I'm going to go inside and poke around a bit," she whispered. "Yasmine, you stand out here and keep guard. Bess and George, you walk down the street a little way. If you see either

Madame Destiny or Dmitri, come tell Yasmine. And, Yasmine, it'll be your job to get me out in time."

"But I don't know what Madame Destiny or Dmitri looks like," George pointed out.

"I'll fill you in," Bess told her cheerfully. "You, too, Yasmine. You can't miss them—especially her."

Nancy proceeded slowly into Madame Destiny's shop. It was so quiet inside, she was convinced it was truly vacant. But just in case she bumped into Madame Destiny or Dmitri in one of the back rooms, she had a story ready. She would confront them about the strange red tea and accuse them of poisoning her.

She opened the door to Madame Destiny's consulting room. It was pitch-black inside. "Hello?" Nancy whispered.

She took a flashlight out of her purse and flicked it on. The room appeared to be empty.

She walked through to the next room beyond. It was cramped and musty-smelling, and lined with dusty, rickety wood shelves. On the shelves were jars full of dry green leaves or gnarled roots. There was even a small cage with live spiders in it.

"Ick!" Nancy said, recoiling instinctively. "What are these. her pets?"

She pointed her flashlight at the spiders. There

were two of them, both fawn-colored, with strange violin-shaped marks on their backs.

Then something else caught her eye. Against one wall was a portable stove. And on top of the stove was a pan filled with a reddish liquid.

It looked like the tea she'd drunk!

Nancy turned and found a light switch. "I'll just turn it on for a minute," she muttered. She leaned over to peer more closely at the pan. Then she picked it up and sniffed at it. It smelled exactly like her tea.

"Nancy?" Yasmine's face suddenly appeared in the doorway.

Nancy started and set the pan down with a clatter. "You scared me," she said breathlessly. "Are Madame Destiny and Dmitri coming?"

Yasmine shook her head. "I got worried about you, that's all." She glanced at the shelves warily. "This place is creepy."

Nancy turned back to the stove. Then she noticed a large leaf on the counter beside it. "Hey, what's this?" she said, picking it up. "It looks like one of those weird greens Hannah likes to cook." She brought it closer to her face, to try to identify it.

The next thing she knew, Yasmine was grabbing it out of her hand. "No!" she cried out. "You'll die if you eat that!"

9

Too Many Suspects

"What do you mean, I'll die?" Nancy exclaimed, staring wide-eyed at Yasmine. "What is it?"

"It's a rhubarb leaf," Yasmine explained. "We studied them in my plant biology class a few weeks ago. They're incredibly poisonous."

"A rhubarb leaf?" Nancy repeated, puzzled. "But rhubarbs are edible."

"That's the scary thing," Yasmine said. "People think that just because you can eat rhubarb stalks—like in rhubarb pie or something—you can eat their leaves, too. But it's totally not true."

Nancy glanced down at the pan of reddish liquid. "This is the tea Madame Destiny fed me earlier," she said slowly. "Say she threw in one of these leaves while she was making the stuff. Would that explain the symptoms I had this afternoon?"

"Definitely," Yasmine said immediately. "And it's a good thing you only had a sip. If you'd had any more, you'd be in intensive care right now."

Nancy was silent as she mulled over this information. It certainly looked as if Madame Destiny was her poisoner. Clearly the fortune-teller wanted to stop Nancy from finding something out. Was it the evil curse scam?

"*Nancy!*" Bess's voice came from the other room in a loud, urgent whisper.

"What?" Nancy softly called back.

"I just spotted Madame Destiny and Dmitri—in that diner you and I went to yesterday," she heard Bess reply. "They're paying their check right now. Come on, you'd better get out of there." Bess added, "Is Yasmine with you?"

"Yes," Nancy said quickly. "Come on, Yasmine, let's go."

But on the way out, Nancy couldn't resist pausing at the desk in the reception area and scanning it quickly. On top of it lay a copy of that day's newspaper and a handful of loose coins.

She also saw half a dozen ticket stubs, all from a parking garage in Chicago called Wally's. Leafing through them hastily, Nancy noted that their dates were all exactly seven days apart. The most recent one was dated the previous Tuesday afternoon.

Someone must be visiting Chicago every Tuesday for some reason, Nancy thought. She didn't know how it might fit in, but just in case, she scribbled down the garage's address on a piece of paper and slipped it into her purse.

As soon as the three girls got outside, George came racing up to them. "They're coming around the corner!" she whispered frantically.

Nancy glanced around, then pointed to a narrow alley between Madame Destiny's shop and the next building. "Over there!"

They slipped into the alley just in time. Seconds later they heard Madame Destiny and Dmitri approach the shop and then go inside, speaking in muffled voices.

Nancy held up her hand, indicating to her friends to wait until the coast was clear. For a couple more minutes they crouched silently in the dark alley. Then they walked out to the street. They went the long way around the block to their car, so they wouldn't pass the shop again.

After they had climbed back in the Mustang, Nancy told Bess and George about the rhubarb leaf.

"So we now have a pretty solid piece of evidence against Madame Destiny; she tried to poison me with that tea," she finished. "It's all beginning to add up: the fact that Madame Destiny tried to scare me with the Death card, and the fact that Frances left an envelope full of cash at her shop yesterday—maybe other Saturdays, too."

George spoke up. "I don't want to be difficult or anything, but do we know for sure that Frances isn't just one of Madame Destiny's clients? I mean, maybe the cash was for a tarot card reading."

"It doesn't fit," Nancy replied, shaking her head. "Four hundred dollars is way too much for any kind of reading. I was only charged ten dollars for my reading. And if Frances is just a customer, why did she freak out when I told her I was paying Madame Destiny a visit?

"Besides," Nancy added, "if Madame Destiny's innocent, why is she so afraid of me?"

As the girls drove home, Nancy mulled over the case in silence. She felt as though she were closing in on Madame Destiny, but at the same time she was frustrated by the number of gaps and missing links in this case.

She couldn't tie Madame Destiny to the bleed valve tampering or to the threatening phone call she'd received late the night before. And unless she could get Frances to open up, she had no way to prove that the fortune-teller was even a con artist.

Besides, how did Dmitri, Loretta, and the red-haired stranger in the gray sedan fit in? And what if Craig wasn't telling her the whole truth about how he'd been acting?

* * *

On Monday morning Nancy's health was back to normal, although her appetite was still a little off. She managed to force down a small piece of dry toast and a glass of milk, but that was all she could take.

While she was in the kitchen, Nancy put in a call to Chief McGinnis's office. Fortunately, the police chief was in. Nancy explained quickly that she needed his help in obtaining a copy of Jake Kittredge's death report from the Lake Sacandaga Village police department.

"Jake Kittredge, eh?" Chief McGinnis said thoughtfully. "I know something about that case, since he was a River Heights resident. It was ruled an accident, you know."

"But what about the fact that his body was never found?" Nancy asked curiously. "And wasn't he supposed to be a good swimmer?"

"According to his wife, yes," Chief McGinnis said. "But the waters were very choppy that day—high winds and all that. The police up there figured he slipped and fell on the deck of his boat, hit his head, and went overboard.

"And as for the business about his body never being found," the chief added, "Sacandaga is an enormous lake, you know. There was another drowning there, two years ago—a woman out sailing alone in bad weather. Her body was never found, either."

Nancy digested this information. It sounded

plausible to her, but she thought it might be a good idea for her to take a look at the report anyway. She asked Chief McGinnis if that would be possible.

"No problem," the chief told her. "It might take a few days, though. They're kind of slow up there."

After thanking him, Nancy hung up and started putting her breakfast dishes in the dishwasher. Just then the phone rang. She wiped her hands on a dish towel and then answered it. "Hello?"

"Nancy, is that you? It's Craig Chandler."

"Oh, hi, Craig," Nancy said. She was surprised to hear from him. "What's up?"

"I'm at Sperry's," he said, then lowered his voice. "I just thought you'd like to know—that housekeeper of Frances's is having breakfast here. I recognize her from times I've visited Frances with Yasmine. Anyway, she's with a young guy who sounds foreign. He's got curly brown hair, green eyes, sort of skinny. They're at one of my tables, and I heard them mention Madame Destiny's name."

Nancy gripped the phone tighter. "That must be Dmitri," she said eagerly. But what on earth was he doing with Loretta? she wondered to herself.

"Did Loretta recognize you, Craig?" Nancy asked him.

"If she did, she sure didn't act like it," Craig replied.

"Listen, I'm coming right over," Nancy said. "In the meantime, any eavesdropping you could do would be greatly appreciated."

"You've got it," Craig said, chuckling. "Hey, if I can't solve the case myself, at least I can help you solve it. See you soon."

But when Nancy got to Sperry's, it turned out that she'd just missed Dmitri and Loretta. "They left about two minutes ago," Craig told her apologetically. "I tried to stall them by being slow with the check, but I guess I didn't stall long enough."

"I'm sure you did your best," Nancy said, trying to bite back her disappointment.

Craig waved his hand at a booth. "You want some coffee or something? I could sit with you for a bit; business is pretty slow this morning."

"Coffee would be great," Nancy said.

Craig disappeared into the kitchen and came back with two steaming white mugs. He plunked them down on the table. "Not poisoned—I promise," he said, smiling as Nancy glanced warily at her mug.

She looked at him and grinned. "Thanks," she said. "So, what did Loretta and Dmitri have to say?"

"I wasn't able to hear too much of their conversation," Craig began. "They were whispering the whole time, and whenever I came by they shut up. I did pick up a few things, though."

Nancy leaned forward. "What?"

"At one point the guy—Dmitri, right?—said to Loretta, 'You must tell me everything you know.'" Craig sipped his coffee. "Then later I heard him saying, 'She's soft. It's all up to you.'"

"'She'—who's 'she'?" Nancy said with a frown. "Madame Destiny? Frances?"

Craig shrugged. "I wish I could tell you. Anyway, that's all I've got for you. I hope it helps."

"I'm sure it will," Nancy said.

They talked for a little while longer, then Nancy stood up to leave. "Thanks for the good detective work, Craig. And thanks for the coffee."

"It's the least I can do," Craig replied with a smile.

Walking out into the cool gray morning, Nancy thought about what Craig had told her. Loretta must be working with Dmitri—and, presumably, Madame Destiny. That could explain why Loretta seemed to have money to spend on nice clothes and jewelry.

But what did Dmitri mean by the words "she's soft"? Nancy wondered. Could he have been talking about Frances? Was he asking Loretta to persuade her employer to fork over more money to Madame Destiny? Who *was* Dmitri, anyway?

Nancy decided to drop by Frances's house and

97

see the elderly woman. It was time to confront her directly about Madame Destiny.

The older woman opened the door when Nancy rang the bell. She peered suspiciously over the rim of her silver reading glasses.

"Hello," Frances murmured, pushing her glasses up her nose. "I'm sorry, dear, but I don't have time for a visit. Loretta's out doing the shopping, and I'm in the middle of—"

"It'll just take a minute, Mrs. Kittredge," Nancy said quickly. "I need to talk to you. It's very important."

Frances stared at her curiously. "Come in, then. Just for a bit, though. I'm busy."

Frances led her into the den. "I was just sorting through some of Jake's papers," she said. "Loretta offered to do it, but I wanted to do it myself, you know? He would have preferred that."

"I'm sure you're right," Nancy murmured sympathetically.

After they were seated, Frances took her glasses off and laid them on her lap. "Now, what was so important? I must say this is all very peculiar. I mean, I hardly know you, young lady."

"I realize that," Nancy said, nodding. She hesitated for a moment before saying, "Listen, I hope you don't think I'm being too personal. But I need to ask you why you were in Madame Destiny's shop on Saturday."

Frances's mouth dropped open. "Madame Destiny's shop?" she repeated, her voice quavering slightly. "I don't know what you're talking about."

"I saw you go in there, Mrs. Kittredge," Nancy said patiently. "Please, you have to level with me. I have good reason to think that you're in trouble."

"In trouble?" Frances exclaimed. Then she lurched forward and started coughing violently.

Nancy touched her shoulder. "Mrs. Kittredge?" she said anxiously. "Mrs. Kittredge, are you okay? Can I get you a glass of water?"

In reply, Frances clutched her chest and cried out in pain. She looked as though she was having a heart attack!

10

Hannah to the Rescue

Nancy looked around frantically for a phone. "Don't worry, Mrs. Kittredge, I'm going to get you a doctor."

Just then she heard the front door open and slam shut. Seconds later Loretta came racing into the den. She had several bags of groceries in her arms.

"Frances?" Loretta said worriedly. "What's going on?"

Frances looked up and pointed at Loretta with a shaking finger. "My pills," she whispered hoarsely. "The yellow ones. They're on the kitchen counter, by the begonia plant."

Loretta dropped the groceries on the coffee table and went running off. When she came back, she had a tall glass of water in her hand.

She knelt beside Frances's hunched-over figure

and held a yellow pill to her lips. "Here, Frances," Loretta said soothingly, then offered her the water. "Drink this. There, you're gonna be all better now."

As Frances gulped down the water, Loretta watched her carefully. Nancy sat down on the couch and did the same.

Seeing Loretta tend to Frances, Nancy felt torn. On one hand, Loretta seemed to be part of the plot to con Frances. On the other hand, Loretta's kind, caring actions seemed to show that she was truly concerned about the elderly woman's well-being.

Gradually Frances's coughing subsided, and her breathing returned to normal.

"I feel much better now," Frances said finally, smoothing her silvery gray curls with her hands. "I'm sorry if I scared anyone. I got a little overexcited, that's all." She stole a quick, nervous glance at Nancy.

Loretta seemed to notice this. Straightening up, she faced Nancy. "If anybody should be sorry, it's you," she said in a huff. "What'd you do—scare poor Frances with stories about your car accident or something?"

"Of course not," Nancy replied. "All I said was—"

"Never mind what you said," Loretta cut in brusquely. "You'd better scoot on out of here. Frances needs peace and quiet."

Nancy stood up. "I hope you feel better, Mrs. Kittredge," she murmured. Neither Frances nor Loretta said anything to her as she walked out the door.

When Nancy got home, she went to her room to think about the case. She was troubled by what had happened at Frances's house. Frances was not in good health—that was obvious. Nancy felt guilty, too, since her questions about Madame Destiny seemed to have brought on the elderly woman's near attack.

Then another, even more disturbing thought crossed her mind. If Madame Destiny had tried to poison Nancy, could she be poisoning Frances, too?

Nancy shook her head. That didn't make sense. Why would Madame Destiny want to hurt Frances? Besides, Frances had seemed fine on Saturday afternoon after leaving the fortune-teller's shop.

One thing was for sure, Nancy thought. She would have to get the goods on Madame Destiny without Frances's cooperation. She couldn't risk upsetting the older woman again.

There was a soft knock on her door, then Hannah poked her head in. "How are you feeling?"

"Much better, thanks," Nancy replied. "You want some help with lunch?"

"It's all taken care of," Hannah said, stepping into the room. "I decided to splurge and buy some lobster salad at that fancy new store, The Golden Gourmet. I felt like a millionaire shopping there, it was so—"

Nancy sat up suddenly. "That's it! Hannah, you're brilliant!"

Hannah broke into a pleased smile. "I am? Well! I ought to buy lobster salad more often, then."

Nancy laughed. "No, no. You gave me an idea for solving this case. And you're going to help me do it."

"Me?" Hannah repeated. "I don't understand, Nancy. How can I possibly help you solve a mystery?"

Nancy jumped out of bed and put her hands on Hannah's shoulders. "First, I want you to go to your closet and get out that beautiful green wool suit of yours. Then go to your jewelry box and fish out your pearl necklace. . . ."

An hour later Hannah stood in the living room dressed in an elegant outfit. In addition to the pearls, she'd set off her suit with a pair of mocha brown suede pumps, a matching purse, and a delicate diamond-studded watch.

Nancy stood back and judged Hannah's appearance. "Looks pretty good. The gizmo doesn't show at all." She then stepped forward and lifted the hem of the housekeeper's jacket. Strapped to Hannah's waist, over her cream-colored silk blouse, was a small black tape recorder.

"This thing is voice-activated," she explained to Hannah. "It should pick up every word of your conversation with Madame Destiny."

Hannah nodded. She looked a little overwhelmed. "Now, let me get this straight," she said slowly. "I'm recently widowed, and I'm very rich—"

"Yes, but don't tell her you're very rich," Nancy interrupted. "Drop some hints. Tell her you just got back from a six-month trip around the world, and it didn't do anything for your grief—or something like that."

"Got it," Hannah said.

"With any luck, Madame Destiny will say there's a curse on you, then ask you for a whole bunch of money. And we'll have it all on tape!" Nancy grinned. "Now come on—let's have some lobster salad before we send you on your way."

Nancy paced almost the entire time while Hannah was gone. She was excited about her plan. If Madame Destiny would try to con anyone, it would be an older, rich-looking widow. Yet she was worried, too. After all, Madame Destiny was dangerous. There was no telling what

104

she might do if she discovered the tape recorder concealed under Hannah's jacket.

When Nancy heard Hannah's car pull into the driveway late in the afternoon, she breathed a sigh of relief. Hannah came through the door a few minutes later.

"Well, that was fun," Hannah announced cheerfully. "I must say, your Madame Destiny is quite a character. That black veil—and those nails!"

"So did she try to con you?" Nancy said eagerly. "Did she ask you for a lot of money?"

"Well, not really," Hannah replied, putting her purse down on the hall table. "Here, why don't you hear it from the horse's mouth? You'll see what I mean."

Nancy unstrapped the tape recorder from Hannah's waist. Then the two of them sat down in the living room and played back the tape.

Nancy noticed that Madame Destiny was giving Hannah the same basic spiel she'd given Nancy on Saturday—throwing around vague, general remarks that could apply to just about anyone.

Then one comment caught Nancy's attention. "I see that there is a great financial opportunity in your very near future, Hannah Gruen," Madame Destiny's theatrical voice came through on the tape. "You must act on it without fail."

Nancy pushed the Pause button. "'A great financial opportunity,'" she repeated thoughtfully.

"That's the only mention she made of money during the entire reading," Hannah told Nancy.

"Interesting," Nancy mused. "I wonder what it means?" She added, "It's also interesting that she asked you your name right off the bat. She never asked me mine."

The phone rang just then. Nancy ran to the kitchen to pick it up. "Hello?"

"Hi, it's Yasmine," Nancy heard her friend say. "I just took a killer chemistry quiz, and I'm about to leave for the animal shelter. How's it going?"

"Fine," Nancy replied, then brought her up to date on the case.

Yasmine was distressed to hear about Frances's near attack. "I don't understand," she murmured anxiously. "She used to be so healthy."

"Really?" Nancy asked her.

"I never knew her to have even a cold, much less heart trouble," Yasmine said. She paused, then added, "I guess she must have gone downhill since Jake died."

The two girls chatted for a minute longer, agreed to talk again soon, then hung up. Nancy went back to the living room. "As I was saying, Hannah, this money business—" she began.

The phone rang again. "I'll get it this time,"

Hannah said, jumping up from the couch and heading for the kitchen.

A few seconds later, Nancy heard Hannah saying in a loud voice, "I'm sorry, this is a terrible connection. Can you please call me back?"

Then Hannah appeared in the living room doorway, flushed with excitement. "When the phone rings, Nancy, pick it up in your father's study. But be very quiet, and don't say a word."

Nancy frowned. "What? What's going on, Hannah?"

The phone began ringing. "Remember, don't say a word," Hannah reminded Nancy as she rushed back to the kitchen.

Confused, Nancy went into her father's study and picked up the phone.

"Is this better, Ms. Gruen?" It was a soft-spoken male voice with a German accent.

"Oh, yes," Hannah replied. "There was all this static on the line before. I couldn't understand a word. Now, who did you say you were again?"

"I'm Dieter von Hallburg," the man said. "I represent the Midas Investment Group."

Nancy's eyes widened as she realized who the man was. His name wasn't Dieter von Hallburg—it was Dmitri!

11

The Chicago Connection

Nancy's mind raced as she realized what this meant. Madame Destiny was indeed a con artist, and she and Dmitri were peddling phony financial investments!

"I hope this is a convenient time to call, Mrs. Gruen," Dmitri was saying. "If not, I'll be happy to call you back at another time. You see, what I have to offer you is so important that I would like nothing less than your full attention."

"Now is fine, I suppose," Hannah replied. "Just what is it you want to talk to me about, Mr.—von Haller, was it?" Nancy was glad to note that Hannah sounded carefully skeptical. Dmitri would get suspicious if Hannah was too enthusiastic about his call.

"Von Hallburg," Dmitri corrected her pleasantly. "You see, the Midas Group is offering shares in a new investment opportunity. And we are inviting discriminating investors like yourself, Mrs. Gruen—may I call you Hannah?—to get in on the action."

"I see," Hannah replied slowly. "Um, can you tell me more about it?"

Dmitri went on to outline a no-risk, surefire plan, guaranteed to make Hannah a fortune. As Nancy listened, she searched her father's desk for a piece of paper and a pen. She wrote in large letters: "Ask to meet in person at his office to discuss. If he says no, suggest a public place like the River Inn. Don't let him come here!"

Nancy put the phone down gently, then tip-toed to the kitchen. She thrust the note at Hannah, who scanned it quickly while murmuring, "Uh huh . . . oh, really?" to Dmitri.

When Nancy got back on the phone in her father's study, Dmitri was saying, "Ten o'clock on Wednesday in the lobby of the River Inn, then. I look forward to meeting you, Hannah."

"I'm not making any promises, but what you've described sounds very interesting," Hannah told him. "I'll bring my checkbook, just in case."

"Very good," Dmitri said. "Wednesday, then. Goodbye."

After hanging up, Nancy rushed to the kitchen. Hannah's face was pink with excitement. "Did I do all right?" she asked Nancy.

Nancy hugged Hannah. "You did great! How

did you know to get me on the phone, by the way?"

"Well, you and I were just talking about Madame Destiny predicting a financial opportunity for me in the very near future," Hannah explained. "Then this man calls, saying he's with an investment company. It seemed too bizarre to be a coincidence."

"Hannah, you have the instincts of a first-rate detective," Nancy complimented her. "That man, Mr. von Hallburg, was Madame Destiny's assistant, Dmitri."

"The quiet fellow with the curly hair?" Hannah said in astonishment. "Oh, my. I had no idea!"

"That's probably because he changed his accent," Nancy said. She crossed her arms, thinking. "So that's their scam. When Madame Destiny gets a rich-looking customer, particularly an older widow, she 'predicts' a money-making opportunity for her. Then Dmitri follows up with a call, posing as a financial adviser. That's why Madame Destiny asked you for your name, Hannah, so they could get your number from the—"

Nancy stopped and gasped. "Edwina Leidig! I wonder if she's one of their victims, too."

"You mean your father's client?" Hannah said.

Nancy nodded and grabbed the phone book. She dialed Edwina's number, and moments later a female voice answered.

110

"Is Edwina there, please?" Nancy asked.

"She's not here," the woman replied politely. "May I take a message?"

"Do you know when I can reach her?" Nancy asked. "This is Nancy Drew. My dad's her lawyer."

"She's been in Chicago since yesterday, visiting friends," the woman replied. "She'll be back tomorrow morning. I'm cat-sitting for her."

Nancy thanked her, then hung up and turned to Hannah. "Well, Edwina's gone till tomorrow, so that will have to wait. In the meantime I'll help you start dinner, and we can plan what you'll say to Dmitri on Wednesday."

Hannah glanced down at her green suit and chuckled. "Sure, Nancy. Just let me get out of my spy outfit and back into my cooking clothes."

The next morning at ten, Nancy picked up Bess and George, and they headed for Edwina Leidig's house. On the way, she filled them in on the events of the day before.

"Why does all the exciting stuff have to happen on the day George and I happened to be painting her bedroom?" Bess grumbled.

"You mean, on the day *I* happened to be painting my bedroom and *you* happened to be reading magazines on my bed," George teased.

Bess shot her a dirty look. "I was scouting decorating tips for you."

111

Nancy grinned. "In any case, guys, the mystery isn't solved yet. I'm sure there's lots more exciting stuff in store for us."

A few minutes later, Nancy turned onto Edwina's street and pulled up in front of her house. Edwina was in the garden, snipping chrysanthemums with a pair of shears.

Edwina rose when she saw the girls get out of Nancy's car. "Oh, hello," she called out, peeling off her gardening gloves. "I hope this means you're ready to start tracking down my Mr. Whittle, Nancy."

"Actually, there's a chance I may have already found him," Nancy replied.

Edwina's eyes grew large. "What?"

"One question, Edwina," Nancy said. "Did you happen to go to a fortune-teller named Madame Destiny before you got the first call from Mr. Whittle?"

Edwina's mouth dropped open. Then she stared down at the bunch of chrysanthemums in her hand. "I—that is, yes, I did," she said after a moment.

Nancy felt a tingle of excitement. "Go on," she said eagerly.

"I was too embarrassed to tell anybody, including the police, that I'd acted on the advice of a fortune-teller," Edwina continued. "Madame Destiny told me I had to seize a golden financial opportunity that would be coming my way soon.

So when Mr. Whittle called me the next day . . ." Her voice trailed off, and she blushed deeply.

Bess laid a hand on Edwina's arm. "It's not your fault," she murmured sympathetically. "Those creeps were taking advantage of you."

"Did you meet with Mr. Whittle face-to-face?" Nancy asked Edwina.

Edwina nodded. "He was a young blond man with glasses. Soft voice. He sounded kind of English to me." She frowned. "Or maybe Irish."

Bess turned to Nancy. "That couldn't have been Dmitri, then. He doesn't wear glasses, and he's definitely not blond."

"He could have been wearing a disguise," Nancy pointed out. "He would have had to. Otherwise Edwina would have recognized him from Madame Destiny's shop."

Edwina looked shocked. "Are you saying that Madame Destiny's young assistant is Mr. Whittle?"

"It's a strong possibility," Nancy replied.

"My goodness," Edwina said.

Nancy asked Edwina a few more questions, then said, "I need a little more evidence before I give Madame Destiny's and Dmitri's names to the police. I'll keep you posted, Edwina. With any luck, you'll have your money back soon."

Edwina thanked her, and the girls turned to go. "What evidence do you still need?" George asked Nancy as they got into the Mustang.

113

Nancy reached in her purse for her keys. "Well, we know what Madame Destiny and Dmitri are up to now," she said. "But I still need proof that Frances Kittredge is one of their targets. Plus, there's the matter of Loretta. . . ."

She frowned suddenly. "Something is bugging me, though. Frances doesn't quite fit into the picture."

"What do you mean, Nan?" Bess asked.

"We saw her taking money to Madame Destiny at her shop," Nancy pointed out. "That doesn't make sense. Madame Destiny's scheme rests on her clients *not* realizing her connection to Mr. Whittle—or Mr. von Hallburg, or whoever Dmitri pretends to be."

"Hmm—you're right," Bess agreed.

Just then Nancy felt a scrap of paper in her purse. Curious, she fished it out. On it was scribbled the address of Wally's Parking Garage in Chicago—the address she'd found on the parking stubs Sunday night at Madame Destiny's shop.

"Hey, guys," Nancy said. "How about a little trip to Chicago?"

"Chicago?" Bess said eagerly. "You mean, like for some shopping?"

"No, I mean for work," Nancy said, chuckling. "I found some parking stubs in Madame Destiny's shop on Sunday night, from a garage in Chicago. They were all dated for Tuesday afternoons. Well, today is Tuesday. I'd like to see if either Madame Destiny or Dmitri makes weekly trips to Chicago—"

"And if it's connected to their scam," George finished.

Nancy grinned. "You got it."

"I thought we were going to Chicago," Bess grumbled.

The three of them were sitting in Nancy's car down the street from Madame Destiny's shop. It was nearly noon, and they'd been there for an hour.

"We don't want to go to Chicago unless either Madame Destiny or Dmitri does, too," Nancy told her. She craned her head to see past a young couple who'd paused in front of the fortune-teller's door.

The couple moved on. Just then Madame Destiny emerged from her shop. She had shed her black robe and veil and was wearing instead an ordinary rust-colored dress and a beige raincoat. She got into a green two-door sedan that was parked nearby.

Nancy started her car. "Here we go," she said, her blue eyes sparkling.

Madame Destiny made her way through town to the highway that led to Chicago. Once on the highway, Nancy followed at a discreet distance, always keeping several cars between them.

About ten minutes into the drive, Nancy noticed a familiar sight in her rearview mirror. It was the red-haired man in the gray sedan!

Who is he? Nancy wondered curiously. If he was working for Madame Destiny, why wasn't he in her car with her?

Nancy glanced in the rearview mirror again. She saw the man talking to himself, looking angry. Then a few minutes later, he pulled off at a rest stop and headed for the gas station.

He's running low on gas! Nancy thought, instinctively peering at her own gas gauge, which showed half-full. One less suspect to worry about, she told herself, refocusing her attention on Madame Destiny's green car.

Two hours later, Madame Destiny reached a slightly run-down residential neighborhood and pulled into Wally's Garage. Nancy parked around the corner, keeping the garage in view. The girls sat in the car and waited.

Madame Destiny came out of the garage a few minutes later. Nancy watched her as she walked purposefully toward an old apartment building across the street.

Nancy turned to Bess and George. "You guys stay here," she said. "I'm going to follow Madame Destiny. I'll be less conspicuous if I'm alone."

"Be careful, Nan," Bess said.

As Nancy crossed the street, she watched Madame Destiny go inside the apartment building's wide glass door. Nancy could easily see through the glass door into the foyer, and through another glass door into the front hall beyond. She saw Madame Destiny pause in the foyer to ring someone's buzzer, then go through the inner glass door toward an elevator bank.

Nancy ran up to the building and went into the foyer. By then, she saw, Madame Destiny had already stepped into the elevator. Nancy could see the number board above it lighting up: 1, 2, and then 3. She's visiting someone on the third floor, Nancy noted.

Nancy pushed the handle of the inner door. It was locked. She turned to a row of eight narrow metal mailboxes set into one wall of the foyer.

From the labels on the boxes, she saw that there were two apartments on the third floor. Apartment 3A was labeled A. Caliban. Apartment 3B had no name.

Nancy bent down. Through the tiny slits in A. Caliban's mailbox, she could see several fliers and envelopes. There was nothing in 3B's mailbox.

"Just what do you think you're doing?" a loud voice boomed behind her.

Nancy whirled around. She'd been so intent on what she was doing, she hadn't noticed anyone come into the building.

117

A shiver of fear went up her spine.

Standing in the open doorway was a tall, muscular man wearing a dirty white T-shirt and overalls. His lips were curled in a menacing sneer, and he held an enormous wrench in one hand, poised in midair.

12

A Ghost Comes to Life

"Didn't hear me the first time?" the guy barked, moving closer to Nancy. "What are you doing here? I'm the building superintendent, and I don't like strangers on the property."

Nancy took a step backward. "I, um, came by to see a friend of mine in 3A," she said quickly. "But he's not home."

"Alonso?" the super said, frowning. The hand holding the wrench dropped to his side. "What do you want to see him for?" He squinted at Nancy's face. "You're kind of young to be hanging out with him, aren't you?"

Picking up his cue, Nancy said, "He's not really *my* friend. He's more like a friend of the family."

"Uh-huh," the super said skeptically. "And

tell me—why were you scoping out his mailbox like that?"

"When he didn't answer his buzzer, I thought he might be out of town or something," Nancy said, improvising. "I wanted to see if his mail was piling up, like if he was away."

Just then the beeper clipped to the super's belt went off noisily. He reached behind and switched it off. "It's probably Mrs. Wasserman up in 2B calling me," he muttered. "Her sink's always backing up."

He pointed his wrench at Nancy and shook it for emphasis. "Listen, kid, if Alonso's not home, why don't you just go on your way?"

Nancy glanced at the wrench. "No problem," she said with an uneasy smile. "I was just leaving, anyway."

Without waiting for the super's reply, she slid past him and out the front door of the building.

Once outside, Nancy paused and took a deep breath, then headed for the blue Mustang. Bess and George were leaning against the car, talking animatedly about something.

George spotted Nancy first. "What happened?" she called out.

Nancy walked up to them and set her purse down on the hood of the car. "I made a new friend," she said dryly. She filled her friends in on the details of her encounter with the super in the foyer.

"Whew! You really talked your way out of that one," Bess said when Nancy had finished. "So which apartment on the third floor do you think Madame Destiny was going to visit? Is there someone in apartment 3B who just doesn't have his name on the mailbox? Or was she going to see this Alfonso whatchamacallit?"

"Alonso," Nancy corrected her. "Which apartment was she visiting? It's hard to say. I'd love to get in that building and snoop around on the third floor, but it's too risky with that super hanging around."

"So what do we do now?" George asked.

Nancy checked her watch. It was almost two-thirty. "I guess we're going to sit in the car and wait for Madame Destiny to come back out," she decided.

That took a lot longer than Nancy had anticipated. An hour passed, then an hour and a half, and still there was no sign of Madame Destiny. Nancy, Bess, and George killed time by discussing the details of the case. At one point, George ran up the street to a corner deli and bought them submarine sandwiches for lunch, since they hadn't had a chance to stop on the way to Chicago.

At around four, Nancy bought a newspaper from a coin box in front of Wally's Garage and brought it back to the car. When George reached

121

out to take the comics page, Bess grabbed it out of her hands.

"Hey, that's mine!" Bess cried out. "You take the sports section—don't you want to read about batting averages or something?"

"Baseball season's over, you dope," George teased. "And aren't you forgetting that—"

"Guys, look!" Nancy said suddenly, interrupting their banter.

Madame Destiny was coming out of the apartment building. Walking with her was a tall man with short gray hair and a mustache. Nancy guessed that he was in his late sixties.

Even from a distance, he looked vaguely familiar to Nancy. She searched her memory. Where had she seen him before?

The man and Madame Destiny crossed the street. They paused at the same coin box where Nancy had been just minutes before, and he bent down to buy a newspaper. Then they waved goodbye to each other, and Madame Destiny headed into Wally's Garage. The man went back across the street and returned to the apartment building.

"I wonder if that could be Alonso Caliban," Nancy said out loud. "Or is he the mystery person in 3B?"

Madame Destiny's green car nosed out of the garage, then turned left onto the street and disappeared from view. Nancy started up the Mustang and headed after her.

The sky was growing dark. A fine, misty rain had started to fall, making the pavement shiny and slick.

"I wonder where she's going next—Milwaukee?" Bess grumbled after a few minutes. "Not to complain or anything, but I'm getting kind of tired of sitting in this car."

"It looks like she's going home, Bess," Nancy reassured her friend. She craned her neck to see past the cars between hers and Madame Destiny's. "She's got her right turn signal on, to get onto the highway. And it looks like she's pointed in the direction of River Heights."

It turned out Nancy was right. A couple of hours later, Madame Destiny pulled up in front of her shop and parked the car. She got out, unlocked the store's front door, and disappeared inside. Nancy noticed that the sign on the store's door read Closed.

"I guess we should call it a night," Nancy announced wearily. "Listen, guys, why don't we pick up some Chinese take-out food and head over to my house? Dad's out of town on business, and Hannah's got the night off, so you can keep me company."

"Sounds great," George said enthusiastically, and her cousin nodded in agreement.

123

Half an hour later, the girls were sitting on the Drews' living room floor. White cartons, chopsticks, paper plates, and tiny packets of hot mustard and sweet-and-sour sauce were spread out on the coffee table.

"So was the trip to Chicago a big dud, or what?" Bess said as she cracked apart a pair of wooden chopsticks. "Pass me the moo shu pork, George."

"It wasn't a big dud, exactly," Nancy replied, spooning some fried rice onto her plate. "This guy Madame Destiny was visiting might be part of her operation. When we turn her in, we can tell the authorities about him, too."

Then she frowned. "You know, he looked kind of familiar to me. I wonder if I've seen his picture in the papers or something. Maybe he's a criminal, and he's hiding out."

George bit into a steamed dumpling, then said, "So when do we get to turn in Madame Destiny and Dmitri?"

"Not yet," Nancy said. "We know that the guy who called Hannah yesterday was Dmitri, but we can't prove it. Once she meets with him face-to-face, we'll have him."

"But what about Loretta and that red-haired guy in the gray car?" Bess reminded Nancy. "Don't you want to get them, too?"

"Hopefully Madame Destiny will spill the

124

beans about her whole operation when she's arrested," Nancy said. "If Loretta and the red-haired man are involved, Madame Destiny will probably end up naming them."

"And Edwina Leidig will get her money back," Bess said cheerfully. "And Frances, too."

"Right. Frances." Nancy looked troubled. "But you know, I still can't figure out why she's been taking money to Madame Destiny's shop. Maybe I was right about the evil curse thing, after all. Maybe Madame Destiny had a different con going with Frances."

After they'd finished dinner, the girls cleared away their mess and settled down to watch some television. "There's a really important preseason basketball game on," George said, picking up the remote control. "See, the regular season hasn't started yet, and these two teams don't normally play against each other in their leagues. But they both were in the play-offs last year, and they got some really good draft picks this year—"

Bess grabbed the remote control from her. "Give me that," she said, pouting. "We have to watch something we *all* like."

She started flicking through the channels. "Oh, there's that new comedy about the guy from outer space who becomes a high school teacher. Nope." She switched channels. "Hmm, public television—some Shakespeare thing. Nope." She switched channels again. "Hey, now this is good. It's that movie about the young nobody who falls in love with a famous actress—"

Nancy sat up suddenly. "Oh, my gosh!" she cried out. "I don't believe it!"

"No, it's true," Bess went on blithely. "He sees her in this Broadway play, and just like that he decides she's the woman for him."

Nancy shook her head vigorously. "No, no, Bess, I'm not talking about the movie. I'm talking about the case. I just realized something important."

Bess and George both turned to her expectantly.

"Now I know who Madame Destiny was visiting in Chicago today," Nancy announced.

Bess looked baffled. "Who—Alonso Caliban?"

"No, no," Nancy insisted. "It was Jake Kittredge."

George frowned. "Frances's dead husband?"

"Yes," Nancy said excitedly. "Only he's not dead. He's really alive!"

13

Prisoners

"What?" George looked totally confused. "How did you figure that one out?"

In reply, Nancy leaped to her feet and went over to the bookshelves. "S, S, S," she muttered, scanning the spines of the books. "Here it is." She reached for a thick volume of Shakespeare plays and cracked it open.

"The Tempest," she said, her eyes shining. She sat back down on the floor and pointed at the book. Bess and George peered at it over her shoulder. "The guy in apartment 3A—his name was Alonso Caliban. Well, Alonso and Caliban are characters in *The Tempest.*"

George slapped her forehead. "Right! Frances told us that Jake used to be an amateur actor and that *The Tempest* was his favorite play. That's why

127

he named their boat the *Prospero.* Prospero's a character in *The Tempest,* too!''

"And their dog is Ariel, another character from the play," Nancy added with a grin.

Bess gasped. "So the old guy we saw with Madame Destiny is really Jake Kittredge, living under a false name?"

Nancy nodded. "That's why his face looked familiar to me—from the photo on Frances's piano. He must not have drowned at all. His body was never found, remember?"

George and Bess both still looked confused. "But how is Madame Destiny connected to him?" George asked slowly.

Nancy looked at the floor, thinking. "I'm not sure. But let's find out if the guy really is Jake Kittredge. Maybe then the other parts of the puzzle will fall into place."

"Should I wear my powder blue dress, or my brown suit with the little gold buttons?" Hannah asked Nancy over breakfast.

Nancy took a sip of grapefruit juice. "Go with the brown suit," she suggested. "So you're all set on what to do in the meeting with Dmitri?"

"I think so," Hannah replied, pulling a piece of paper out of her apron pocket. "I wrote it all down." She studied the paper. "I meet him at ten in the River Inn lobby. He pitches his investment idea to me, and I pretend to be very interested. Then I hand him a check for a thousand dollars—"

"Which we'll stop payment on, right after your meeting," Nancy cut in.

Hannah nodded. "Right. And you'll hide behind a column and take a snapshot of Dmitri—"

"Which I'll show to Edwina Leidig. And as soon as she identifies him as Thomas Whittle, we'll turn the whole thing over to the police." Nancy stood up and clapped her hands together. "Terrific. I think this is all going to work."

Hannah put her coffee cup in the sink and rinsed it out. "You'd better not drive with me to the River Inn. Dmitri might see us together."

Nancy shook her head. "I have to run over to Madame Destiny's shop first." She glanced at her watch. "In fact, I'd better get moving or I won't make it to the River Inn on time."

Nancy picked up her purse from the counter and headed for the door. On the way, she stopped to give Hannah a kiss on the cheek. "Good luck. And thanks so much for helping me out on this."

Hannah beamed. "I'm having fun, actually. Now I know why you like being a detective so much!"

Half an hour later, Nancy was sitting in her Mustang with George and Bess. They were parked across the street from Madame Destiny's shop. It was a cool, damp morning, and the dark gray clouds overhead threatened rain.

"You want to find out from Madame Destiny if this Alonso is really Jake, right?" George spoke up from the backseat. "So do you have a plan?"

"Kind of," Nancy said slowly. "But I'll need both you guys in there with me."

Bess made a face. "Just promise me I won't have to drink any poisonous tea."

Nancy chuckled. "I promise."

When the three of them walked into the front door of the fortune-teller's shop, they found Madame Destiny sitting at the desk reading a newspaper. When she saw the girls, she snapped the paper shut and gave them a tense smile. "I'm really not open for business yet—" she began.

Nancy clasped her hands together. "But this is very important," she said anxiously. "I need you to conduct a séance for us right away. I'll pay you anything—anything at all."

Madame Destiny studied Nancy with narrowed eyes. Then she said, "All right. Give me a minute, please." She rose with a swish of her robe and disappeared through the door marked Private. In a few seconds, she called out, "Come in, please."

Nancy went through the door, followed by Bess and George. Madame Destiny's inner room was pitch-black, except for one flickering candle on the main table. She was seated there, eyes half-closed, her hands hovering spookily over her crystal ball. The air was thick with the smell of incense.

"Sit down," she ordered the girls.

Madame Destiny continued to gaze into the crystal ball. Nancy glanced at George, who was staring at the fortune-teller in fascination. Bess, on the other hand, shifted nervously in her chair, her eyes darting around the dark room.

"The name," Madame Destiny said suddenly. Her eyes remained half-closed. "Tell me the name of the deceased person with whom you wish to communicate."

Nancy cleared her throat, then said: "I wish to communicate with Jake Kittredge, also known as Alonso Caliban."

Madame Destiny's reaction was immediate and violent. Her eyes flew open, and she jumped up from her chair, accidentally knocking over the table and the candle. Nancy, Bess, and George scrambled to their feet. The crystal ball flew into the air, landed on the floor, and shattered.

Thinking quickly, Nancy stomped out the candle, then rushed toward Madame Destiny in the darkness. She didn't want the fortune-teller to get away.

But just as Nancy was about to grab her, an overhead light flicked on. Nancy staggered and blinked in the sudden brightness.

"Look out, Nan!" George shouted.

Nancy whirled around. A blond man in a gray suit was coming toward her. He had a switchblade in one hand, poised in the air and ready to strike.

It was Dmitri!

Nancy stepped sideways out of his path. But her foot caught on the leg of Madame Destiny's table, and she tripped and fell to the floor.

Dmitri was upon her in a second. "Just where do you think you're going?" he growled, lifting her roughly off the floor. Without waiting for a reply, he grasped her arm with one hand and held the deadly switchblade to her neck with the other.

Trying to ignore the cold metal against her throat, Nancy stood very still. How could she get away from Dmitri without getting herself hurt?

Then, out of the corner of her eye, she saw George and Bess heading for the door to the reception area, running for help.

"One more step, and Dmitri will put your nosy detective friend out of commission—permanently," Madame Destiny shouted. Her voice didn't sound quite so refined now.

George and Bess froze. They turned and glanced at Nancy helplessly.

Madame Destiny pointed to the chairs lying on the floor. "Pick up a chair and sit down," she ordered George and Bess. "*Now.*"

The girls hesitated for a moment, then obeyed.

While Dmitri still held the switchblade to Nancy's throat, Madame Destiny went into the back storage room. She returned a few seconds later with some twine and rags. She proceeded to bind George to her chair and stuff a rag snugly into her mouth. She did the same with Bess, then finally sat Nancy down and repeated the procedure.

"You girls have become very irritating to me," Madame Destiny muttered as she finished. She crooked a finger at Dmitri. "Come on. We have a lot to do." The two disappeared into the back storage room.

Nancy struggled to free her wrists, but they were bound securely. With a sigh, she settled onto her chair and looked around. In the bright light the fortune-telling room looked small and shabby. The walls were covered with tacky lime green wallpaper, and the cement floor was bare. The only furnishings were the table, chairs, and a wobbly bookshelf that held a tarot deck, candles, and a box of incense.

From the storage room, Nancy could hear the drawers opening and closing, jars clinking together, papers rustling. What were Madame Destiny and Dmitri up to? she wondered. And what did they plan to do with Nancy and her friends?

Nancy soon found out. Ten minutes later the fortune-teller and her assistant emerged from the back room, carrying suitcases.

133

Madame Destiny fixed her eyes on Nancy. "We'd been planning to leave this miserable little town in a few weeks," she sneered. "But thanks to you, we've had to hurry things up a bit. So we're off—maybe to California, maybe Hawaii, maybe South America. I love warm climates." She glanced at Dmitri. "Of course, my dear assistant has one more appointment to keep first."

Nancy realized that Dmitri still planned to meet with Hannah. At least the River Inn lobby was a public place, she told herself. If anything went wrong, there was no way Dmitri could harm Hannah.

Madame Destiny headed for the doorway to the reception area. Then, almost as an afterthought, she stopped and pulled something out of one of her bags. It was the small cage of spiders that Nancy had seen on Sunday night.

She set the cage down on the floor and opened it. "Let me introduce you to my little pets," she said sweetly. "Brown recluses. Their bites are—well, they're quite deadly." She added, "I'd finish you off more quickly, but I do so detest guns and knives. Blood can be so messy."

She gave them a cruel smile. "Enjoy your last few minutes," she said, then flicked the overhead light off and walked through the door. Dmitri followed her, closing the door behind him. A few seconds later, Nancy heard them leaving the shop.

The three girls sat in the eerie darkness. Nancy heard George make a few muffled sounds, but gagged as they were, it was useless to try to talk.

Gradually Nancy's eyes adjusted to the dim light that fell through the crack under the door. She glanced nervously at the spider cage and saw the two fawn-colored spiders wandering out.

Brown recluses, Madame Destiny had called them. Nancy recalled reading about them in some book a long time ago. They were highly dangerous members of the spider family, the book had said.

When Nancy turned to look at Bess, she saw that her eyes were enormous with fear.

Maybe they would get lucky, and the spiders wouldn't bite them, Nancy thought. But she didn't want to take any chances.

Then Nancy saw the light glint off the shattered crystal ball on the floor. She got an idea.

One of the shards was lying close to George. Keeping her eyes on the spiders, Nancy began rocking her chair back and forth, trying to scoot it in the direction of the shard. *Thunk, thunk, thunk.* She moved the chair in short, jerky hops, gasping to breathe around the rag in her mouth.

When she got near the shard, she aimed carefully, then let her chair tip to the right. She landed on the cement floor with a noisy bang. Her right shoulder throbbed painfully from the impact. She was within reaching distance of the shard, though.

But the spiders were less than five feet away from her now.

Determined, Nancy wriggled around until she could pick up the shard with her fingers. She felt a tiny stinging sensation—she'd cut herself against the sharp edge of the glass.

At least that means the edge is sharp enough to cut the twine, she told herself. Gazing up at George, she bobbed her head down toward the floor several times, indicating that George should tip her chair over, too.

George looked uncertain, but she obeyed. She landed next to Nancy with a crash and a loud moan.

Nancy squirmed around so she was back-to-back with George, then began sawing carefully at her friend's bonds with the shard. It worked! In less than five minutes George's wrists were free.

George immediately undid the twine around her ankles, then sat up and untied Nancy.

Nancy leapt up and stomped on the spiders. They lay squashed, less than a foot from where she'd been lying a moment earlier.

Nancy pulled the gag out of her mouth. "George, are you okay?" she said quickly.

George had already taken the rag out of her

own mouth and was busy untying Bess. "I'm fine," she replied. "I've got a few bruises, no big deal."

"Are those spiders really dead?" Bess said in a shaky voice as soon as she'd unstuffed her mouth.

"They're very dead, Bess," Nancy reassured her. "Now we have to get over to the River Inn and stop Dmitri and Madame Destiny."

Just then Nancy heard the front door of the shop open and close. The three girls froze.

"Livvy, is that you back there?" someone called out. "I was driving by, dear, and I saw the Closed sign. What's going on?"

Listening to the familiar voice, a shocking realization dawned on Nancy. She flung open the door to the reception area. There stood Frances Kittredge with a key in her hand.

"You!" Frances cried out, taking a step back.

Nancy stared into Frances's pale blue eyes—the same color as Madame Destiny's.

"You two are sisters, aren't you?" Nancy said slowly.

14

A Deadly Chase

Frances's mouth fell open, then clamped shut. When she finally spoke, her voice was trembling. "What have you done to my sister? What have you done to Livvy?"

"She tried to kill the three of us, then made a run for it," Nancy replied tartly.

Frances's eyes grew wide. Then she turned swiftly and made a move toward the door.

Nancy grabbed her arm. "Not so fast," she warned. "You're staying right here with us."

"I'll call the police," Bess said helpfully, walking over to the desk and picking up the phone. She put her ear to the receiver and frowned. "Hey, there's no dial tone."

George peered down at the phone jack. "No wonder," she said. "The line's been cut."

"There's no time, anyway," Nancy told them. "We've got to get to the River Inn, and fast. Hannah's there with Dmitri right now." She turned to Frances. "You're coming, too. I'm not letting you out of my sight until this is all over."

"What kind of way is this to treat an old woman?" Frances protested. "I'm telling you, I'm innocent!" But she didn't resist as Nancy led her to the Mustang.

Once in the car, Bess and George sat in the backseat with Frances wedged between them, while Nancy drove. They were only a few blocks away from the fortune-teller's shop when the skies opened up and it started to pour. Nancy turned her windshield wipers on, but it was still difficult to see out.

Nancy glanced briefly in the rearview mirror. "So you're partners with your sister and Dmitri in their crooked scheme, huh?" she said to Frances. "And your husband—I suppose he's in on it, too?"

Frances looked startled. "You—you know about Jake?"

"Yup," Nancy replied. "The only thing is, why fake his death? Was he wanted by the police, or—" She stopped suddenly. An important piece of the puzzle had just clicked into place.

"I get it now," she said slowly. "Your plan was to get the life insurance money. Jake pretended to drown and went into hiding, and you played the grieving widow. You were just waiting for a check from the insurance company, right? Then you two were going to move far away and be together again."

Frances leaned forward and put her hands on the back of Nancy's seat. "We weren't doing anyone any harm," she pleaded. "All our lives, we never had much money. We both tried to make it as actors, but that didn't work out. Then Jake got a job teaching drama at a community college. His mother left us our beautiful house, but aside from that, we never had anything nice for ourselves."

"So you thought you'd cheat the insurance company out of a few hundred thousand dollars? Or was it more?" Nancy asked her.

Frances didn't answer her question. "Why shouldn't we enjoy a few luxuries in our old age?" she said stubbornly. "We were going to buy a little condominium in Florida, or maybe New Mexico. And then we were going to go on a Caribbean cruise. How could anyone begrudge us that?"

"Nobody holds it against you for wanting those things," George replied. "But what you did was still against the law."

Nancy was silent. She wanted to grill Frances some more, but the rain was pouring down even harder now, and she had to concentrate on getting to the River Inn in one piece. Hannah needed her.

Five minutes later Nancy pulled up in front of the posh inn. "You guys stay here with Frances," she ordered Bess and George. "I'm going to rescue Hannah, then I'll call the police." She raced out of the car and into the pelting rain, slamming the car door behind her.

She ran into the lobby, wiping her wet hair out of her eyes. Her clothes were soaking, and her right hand bled slightly from where she'd cut it on the crystal shard.

The doorman standing inside the portico looked her up and down. "May I help you, miss?" he said haughtily.

"I—no, thank you," Nancy returned. "I'm looking for someone."

She scanned the crowded lobby, trying to spot Hannah and Dmitri. After a moment she saw them sitting side by side on a velvet couch. Dmitri was showing Hannah some papers, and she was nodding. A silver tea service was laid out on the table in front of them.

Nancy felt relief wash through her. Hannah was okay. Now, if only she could get her away from Dmitri quickly and safely . . .

But just then a tall woman in a bright pink suit rushed up to Hannah. "Hannah dear," she said in a loud, shrill voice. "I haven't seen you in ages. How *are* you?"

Nancy noticed that Hannah turned pale as a ghost. She said something to the woman that Nancy couldn't hear.

"Well, I won't keep you then," the woman went on. She gave Hannah and Dmitri a little wave. "Do give my best to Carson Drew and that daughter of his—Nancy, right? 'Bye now!"

Dmitri put his papers down slowly and stared at Hannah in disbelief.

Oh, no, Nancy thought. Now he knows that Hannah is connected to me!

Hannah didn't waste any time. As her friend in the pink suit turned and headed for the elevators, Hannah grabbed her purse and started to jump up. But Dmitri was too fast for her. Seizing her arm, he yanked her close to him. He pressed something against her with his other hand, hidden under his jacket. It must be a knife or a gun, Nancy realized in horror. Then he forced her onto her feet, and the two of them shuffled toward the inn's side exit.

Her heart pounding, Nancy hurried through the lobby after them. She didn't want Dmitri to see her; one false move, and Hannah might end up getting hurt.

By the time she reached the exit, she saw Dmitri push Hannah into Madame Destiny's green car, which was parked at the curb. Madame Destiny was at the wheel.

Now what? Nancy asked herself frantically.

Then she got an idea. As Madame Destiny drove away into the rain, Nancy made a mental note of her license plate number. Then she doubled back into the lobby and ran up to the haughty doorman.

"One of your customers has just been abducted," Nancy told him breathlessly. She gave a description of the car and scribbled the license plate number on a piece of paper. "Please call the police right away. As far as I can tell, they're headed east along the river."

He stared at her in amazement. "But, miss—"

But Nancy was already on her way out the door. "I'm going to follow them," she called out over her shoulder. "Please, just call the police!"

Nancy sprinted through the rain and got into the Mustang. Her fingers were trembling as she turned on the ignition. If anything should happen to Hannah . . .

"Nancy, what's going on?" George said, leaning forward. "We saw Madame Destiny's car come tearing out of the parking lot."

"They've got Hannah," Nancy said grimly. She put the Mustang in gear, then started down the street, along the river.

"Hannah!" Bess cried out. "Oh, no!"

"The police are on their way," Nancy said. "At least I hope they are. In the meantime, I've got to try to catch them."

Frances looked worried. "This isn't going to

turn into one of those high-speed car chases like on TV, is it?" she asked.

Nancy didn't reply. The rain continued to pour down in sheets, making driving difficult. At least there's no traffic, she told herself.

Three blocks away, Nancy saw the green car up ahead. "There they are!" she cried, stepping on the accelerator a little harder.

"Do you have to drive so fast?" Frances said anxiously. "Maybe you should just let them go." She added, "My sister can be a little hotheaded. If she thought you were interfering with her plans in any way, she might hurt your friend Hannah."

Nancy's chest tightened at Frances's words, but she knew she couldn't let Madame Destiny go now. She had to keep on her tail until the police caught up to them—or else the fortune-teller and Dmitri and Hannah might disappear altogether.

Madame Destiny seemed to know she was being followed, because the green car picked up speed. The street was getting more deserted and desolate. Nancy could see blurry images of old warehouses and barren-looking trees flash by as she drove.

Suddenly a plan popped into Nancy's mind. "Hang on, guys," she said over her shoulder. "Cottage Street is coming up. I'm going to make them turn onto it."

"Cottage Street!" Bess exclaimed. "That dead-ends at the river, doesn't it?"

"Yup. Let's just hope that Madame Destiny doesn't know that." Nancy floored the accelerator.

The Mustang kicked into overdrive. Nancy hated driving so fast, especially in the rain, but she had no choice. She had to save Hannah!

Within thirty seconds Nancy was side by side with the green car. Glancing to the right briefly, she could make out Madame Destiny's grim profile in the driver's seat. Hannah and Dmitri were in the backseat.

Nancy's knuckles were white as they gripped the steering wheel. Cottage Street was just ahead, to the right. She had a nearly impossible maneuver to make, and she had to time it perfectly.

Now! she told herself. She cut in front of the green car, then angled her car and braked. The Mustang fishtailed wildly, then stopped. Madame Destiny reacted instantly with a screeching turn to the right, onto Cottage Street.

"Yes!" Nancy cried out. "It worked!"

"That was *much* worse than those car chases on TV!" Frances complained from the backseat.

Nancy backed up and followed the green car down Cottage Street. It was only a block long, ending at the river. Madame Destiny seemed to realize this right away; she slowed down and tried to make a U-turn. Anticipating this, Nancy stepped on the brake and spun her Mustang sideways, blocking Madame Destiny's exit.

The green car stopped suddenly, then the doors burst open. Madame Destiny jumped out, her eyes flashing dangerously. Dmitri emerged from the back, half-covering his head with his jacket but still holding Hannah close to his side. The housekeeper's face looked deathly white.

Nancy jumped out of the Mustang and faced Madame Destiny. "Let her go," she shouted above the noise of the falling rain. "This is the end of the line for you."

"You're in no position to threaten me, my dear," Madame Destiny spat out wildly. She thrust a pointing finger toward Dmitri and Hannah. Dmitri pulled his switchblade out of his pocket and held it openly against Hannah's throat. The steel blade glinted coldly in the rain.

"See, Nancy Drew," the fortune-teller hissed. "Either you let us go, or you'll be holding a séance for your friend Hannah in the very near future."

15

A Bright and Happy Future

Nancy forced herself to stay calm as she said to Madame Destiny, "And what would your sister think of that?"

"My sister?" Madame Destiny gasped. "What are you talking about?"

Nancy pointed to the back door of the Mustang. Bess and George came out, with Frances pinned tightly between them.

"Frannie!" Madame Destiny cried out. She sounded anxious now and not so sure of herself. "What's going on?"

"Please just let that woman go, Livvy dear," Frances pleaded. "It's no use. The police are on their way."

As she said those words, Nancy heard the wail of sirens in the background.

Madame Destiny and Dmitri exchanged a

glance. Then Dmitri roughly pushed Hannah away and started racing toward the river.

Nancy rushed up to Hannah and pulled her out of Madame Destiny's reach. Then Nancy grabbed the fortune-teller before she could make her escape, too.

"Not so fast, mister!" someone barked out.

Nancy squinted over Madame Destiny's shoulder. A figure had suddenly appeared in the rain, coming toward them from the river.

It was the mysterious red-haired driver of the gray sedan!

"You're not going anywhere," he said as he blocked Dmitri's escape. When Dmitri tried to step around him, the red-haired man grabbed his arm and twisted it around his back.

Dmitri cried out in pain. Then, in one swift motion, the red-haired man tore the switchblade out of Dmitri's grip.

"But I don't get it!" Bess burst out. "You're one of the bad guys! Why aren't you helping out your fellow gang members?"

"Fellow gang members?" The red-haired man shot Bess a puzzled look. "I'm Phil Reynolds. I'm an investigator for the Consolidated Insurance Company. For the last six months I've been looking into Frances Kittredge's million-dollar life insurance claim for her husband."

"An investigator!" George exclaimed, just as

two police cars came screeching down Cottage Street.

"As far as I'm concerned, you did my job for me, Ms. Drew," Phil Reynolds was saying to Nancy. "If it weren't for you, we might never have found Jake Kittredge."

Sitting at the Nassers' dining room table, the insurance investigator cradled a cup of mint tea in his hands. It was Thursday night, and Yasmine had invited everyone over for dinner to celebrate Nancy's solving the case. Nancy, George, and Bess were there, as were Hannah, Craig, and Edwina.

"And if it hadn't been for you, Nancy, I would never have gotten my ten thousand dollars back," Edwina added gratefully.

Chief McGinnis had relayed the final details of the case to Nancy, and she was now sharing the news with her friends. Frances Kittredge had confessed everything to the police the day before.

Olivia Paretsky—otherwise known as Madame Destiny—and her assistant, Dmitri, whose real name was Joey McClain, had claimed to be innocent at first. But after the police went through their suitcases and found so much incriminating evidence, the fortune-telling team confessed, too.

"I still can't believe it." Yasmine sighed and passed around a plate of fruit and pastries. "Frances and Jake." She smiled sadly at Nancy. "Isn't it ironic? I asked you to find the crook who was ripping off Frances, and it turns out she was a crook herself!"

Nancy put her hand on Yasmine's arm. "I'm sorry things worked out this way," she murmured. "You were being so nice, worrying about Frances. But think of it this way—if the Consolidated Insurance Company had paid that million dollars, it would eventually have come out of the pockets of all its honest policyholders."

"That's true," Yasmine admitted. "And I *am* glad that we stopped Madame Destiny and Dmitri from stealing money from any more widows and widowers." She flashed Edwina Leidig a sympathetic smile.

"So Frances had nothing to do with the phony financial investment stuff her sister was doing?" Bess piped up, biting into a cookie.

Nancy shook her head. "Nothing whatsoever. Madame Destiny and Dmitri have been going around the country for the last two years, setting up their fortune-telling shop and then pulling the investment scam on innocent customers. Frances and Jake weren't involved in that in any way. Their little fraud was just a one-time deal."

"The life insurance scam," George put in, nodding. "But what about the envelope of money you saw Frances bring to her sister? What was that for?"

"Madame Destiny was helping Frances out," Nancy explained, dabbing her lips with a linen napkin. "While Consolidated was still investigating Frances's claim, she couldn't risk being seen anywhere near Jake's hiding place. So every week she took money out of the bank and gave it to her sister.

"Then Olivia would take it to Jake in Chicago," Nancy went on, "so he'd have money for his rent, food, and other stuff like that. The Chicago police picked him up yesterday afternoon, by the way."

"What about Loretta?" Craig spoke up.

"It's funny—if it weren't for Loretta, we might have wrapped up this case days ago," Nancy replied. "Last Friday, when George, Bess, Yasmine, and I first visited Frances at her house, Loretta was there. She happened to recognize me from the newspapers and tipped Frances off that I was a detective."

She added, "Then on Saturday, after I bumped into Frances in front of Madame Destiny's shop, Frances called her sister to warn her about me. That's why Madame Destiny suddenly gave me the Death tarot card, to scare me."

"Was Madame Destiny responsible for tampering with your car, or did Dmitri do that?" Bess asked curiously.

151

"Dmitri messed up my bleed valve while you and George and I were having lunch, Bess," Nancy said. "But it was Madame Destiny who called me later that night, with her voice disguised."

"So was Loretta in cahoots with Frances and Jake, too?" Hannah asked her.

Nancy chuckled. "That's right. After all, they paid her a nice salary and gave her free room and board.

"But on top of that," she added, "they had promised her a small cut of the life insurance settlement in exchange for helping out with the scam. You know—keeping quiet, lying to the authorities if necessary, stuff like that. And Loretta was only too happy to cooperate. She's got expensive tastes, and she wanted the money."

Nancy took a sip of mint tea. "That's why she was in front of my house last Saturday evening. She was curious about me, and she wanted to check me out. And on Monday, when Frances pretended to have a heart attack—I was asking her too many questions about Madame Destiny— Loretta played right along. She brought Frances a vitamin pill and pretended it was some sort of medication."

Craig looked confused. "But what about that morning when I saw Loretta meeting with Dmitri at Sperry's? What was that all about?"

"Dmitri called her up and asked to meet with her," Nancy said. "He wanted to grill her about how I'd been poking around at Frances's, stuff like that. Plus, he thought Loretta should do something to stop me—he thought Frances was being too 'soft.'"

Just then there was a faint scratching noise at the back door. "The puppies!" Yasmine cried out, pushing her chair back. "I forgot all about them."

She disappeared into the kitchen, then came back a moment later followed by her three large brown dogs, Izzy, Cleopatra, and Boots. Bringing up the rear was a fourth dog—Ariel.

Bess grimaced. "Oh, no, she followed me here so she could bite me!"

Yasmine laughed. "You two just got off to the wrong start. Really, she's a sweetheart." She extended her hand to Ariel, who licked it happily. "I went over to get her, since the police took Frances and Loretta away," she explained. "Poor thing, she was all alone over there."

Craig put his arm around her. "You have a heart of gold, Yasmine. No wonder I'm so crazy about you."

"Oh, Craig," Yasmine said, pushing him away playfully. But Nancy could see that her eyes were shining.

"I propose a toast," Edwina said suddenly,

raising her tea high in the air. "To Nancy Drew, the world's greatest detective. And her fabulous assistants, George and Bess."

"And Hannah," Bess added. "Not only can she cook a mean pot roast, but she can sniff out crooks with the best of them."

Everyone laughed. "Oh, it was nothing," Hannah said, blushing. "Nancy deserves all the credit."

"Speaking of Nancy . . ." George leaned over and peered into her friend's teacup. "Oh, yes," she said in a spooky tone of voice. "The tea leaves are swirling about. They cast a pattern, a pattern of danger and intrigue. They tell me . . ."

George closed her eyes and appeared to be concentrating hard. "They tell me that there's another case for you in the near future, Nancy Drew." Her eyes popped open as everyone laughed again.

"Now, *that's* my kind of fortune-telling," Nancy replied with a grin.